BORN WEIRD

By the same author

All My Friends are Superheroes
The Waterproof Bible
The Tiny Wife

BORN WEIRD

ANDREW KAUFMAN

The Friday Project
An imprint of HarperCollins*Publishers*
77–85 Fulham Palace Road
Hammersmith, London W6 8JB
www.harpercollins.co.uk

First published in Great Britain by The Friday Project in 2013

1

Andrew Kaufman asserts the moral right to
be identified as the author of this work

A catalogue record for this book
is available from the British Library

ISBN 9780007441402

Text design and images by Leah Springate

Printed and bound in Great Britain by
Clays Ltd, St Ives plc

MIX
Paper from
responsible sources
FSC™ C007454

FSC™ is a non-profit international organisation established to promote
the responsible management of the world's forests. Products carrying the
FSC label are independently certified to assure consumers that they come
from forests that are managed to meet the social, economic and
ecological needs of present and future generations,
and other controlled sources.

Find out more about HarperCollins and the environment at
www.harpercollins.co.uk/green

For Phoenix, Frida and Marlo

W

THE WEIRDS ACQUIRED THEIR SURNAME through a series of events that some would call coincidence and others would call fate.

Sterling D. Wyird, in the process of emigrating from England to Canada, worked his way across the Atlantic aboard the Icelandic fishing trawler *Örlög*. Inclement weather and empty nets made the six-week journey three months long. When Sterling finally stepped onto the freshly built planks of Pier 21 in Halifax he presented his papers to an immigration guard who, just that morning, had met the woman destined to become his wife. This guard, in a stroke of either inspiration or absent-mindedness, changed the *y* in Sterling's last name to an *e*. Seventy-seven years later, as his great-grandchildren gathered for the final game of their high school football team's season, the spelling mistake remained. They were still Weird.

The four oldest siblings—Richard, nineteen; Lucy, seventeen; Abba, sixteen; and Angie, fourteen—were in the stands, ready to watch Kent, the youngest, play football. Or rather to watch Kent sit on the bench as his teammates played football. Kent was in Grade Nine but he'd skipped Grade Six, so he was only thirteen—yet he'd somehow managed to earn a spot as the third-string quarterback. That Kent had spent the season sitting on the bench didn't bother the Weird siblings in the least. They preferred that he should never make it onto the field. The idea of having to watch him play filled them all with anxiety. Which is why the last game of the season was the first they'd come to see.

They stood in the crowd, feeling awkward. Theirs were the only faces not painted blue and white, the school's colours. Their classmates chanted fight songs that they didn't know the words to. But Kent remained safely on the bench.

Then, with fifty-seven seconds left in the game, the team's star quarterback, Kevin Halleck, received a stunning sack and had to be carried off the field. Mike Bloomfield, the second-string quarterback, had just been diagnosed with mononucleosis, and therefore was home. The coach looked at Kent and gave him the nod. Kent ran onto the field for the first time that season, failing to notice that his shoes were untied.

The home team was losing by a field goal. Or, to put it another way, a touchdown would give them the game. The idea that Kent had been given this chance seemed unbelievable to his brother and sisters. It's not as if the Weird children were outcasts. They were popular. They just weren't A-list. To reach the zenith of teenage popularity, at least at

F.E. Madill Secondary School, athletic accomplishment was a non-negotiable prerequisite. The sort of popularity that, should Kent win this game, would instantaneously be transferred on to each of them. Angie was very aware that this was the strange thing about excelling in high school—it made you more normal, not more exceptional. And normalcy was what she craved more than anything else.

But did she yell and cheer for Kent? No, she did not. None of them did. They didn't even call out his name. They were terrified. Not one of them spoke as Kent bent down and tied his shoes. Angie searched the crowd but she couldn't see their mother, father or grandmother. Her parents had gone to the airport, or so she believed, to pick up her grandmother, arriving for her annual month-long Christmas visit. The plan had been for everyone to meet in the parking lot before the game. But her parents and grandmother had never arrived. The thought that they were missing Kent's potential moment of triumph was greatly upsetting to Angie. But then she forgave them, instantly. And as Kent called the play she forgot about them completely.

The teams got into position. The siblings remained silent. The blue and white faces surrounding them cheered their heads off.

"Hut!" Kent called.

The centre flicked the ball into his hands. The clock ticked. Kent went back. He threw a pass. It tumbled through the air and into the stands.

The teams huddled again. Kent clapped his hands. Everyone went into formation. Second down with thirty-six seconds left on the clock. The ball was snapped. Kent faked a pass. Then he handed the football to a running back, who was quickly tackled just behind the line of play. It was a loss of two yards.

Twenty-three seconds were left on the clock, which continued to tick. Last down and last chance. The centre snapped the ball into Kent's hands. His brother and sisters still didn't cheer. They were terrified that Kent was going to drop the football. He took two steps back and then a third. He turned his head to the right and raised the ball but he didn't throw it. Angie glanced at the clock. It ticked down through the number thirteen. When she looked back at Kent, she saw him do a very odd thing: he shut his eyes. They remained closed as he tucked the ball against his chest and began to run.

Their breaths held, Richard, Abba, Lucy and Angie watched Kent as he ran forwards. His head was down. His eyes were still closed. He ran directly into the defensive line. For a moment he disappeared behind opposition uniforms—and then there he was, on the other side.

Less than twenty yards separated Kent and the goal line. At the five-yard line a lanky safety caught up to him. The opposing player leapt into the air. He landed heavily on Kent's back. Kent didn't seem to notice. With the safety's arms wrapped around his waist Kent ran over the goal line and into the end zone.

Kent didn't open his eyes until he heard the roar of the crowd. He saw the cheering fans and his astonished siblings and his overjoyed teammates running towards him. Then he saw his grandmother. She stood at the edge of the field. Her face wordlessly conveyed that something horrible had happened. The ball fell out of Kent's hands just as his teammates reached the end zone. They tried to hoist him on their shoulders. But Kent evaded their grasp. He walked to the sidelines, took off his helmet and approached his grandmother.

And so Kent was the first of the Weirds to learn that everything had changed forever.

Their father was dead.

BOOK ONE:

Blessing + Curse = Blursing

ON APRIL 7, 2010, eight and a half years after Kent scored his first and only touchdown, Angie Weird stood in a hallway on the fourth floor of the Vancouver and District General Hospital, eavesdropping on her grandmother as she dictated her epitaph. "Until you realize that coincidences don't exist, your life will be filled with them," Grandmother Weird said. "Everywhere you look there coincidences will be. Coincidence! Coincidence! Coincidence! But the moment you accept there is no such thing, they will disappear forever and you'll never encounter another."

Angie tried not to vomit. The corridor, in fact the whole hospital, smelled like artificial pine. But her grandmother's ridiculous speech was as nausea-making as the smell of disinfectant. Hearing her grandmother's words reminded Angie of everything she disliked about her family, and why she had avoided all contact with them for so many years. Even though she'd just flown from New York, five and a half hours in the air with a two-hour stopover in Toronto, Angie decided to head back to the airport.

She turned away from her grandmother's hospital room and towards the elevators. It was at this exact moment that an orderly was checking his phone as he pushed a cart down the hall. He did not look up until his shoulder struck Angie's. Knocked off balance, Angie was sent stumbling into her grandmother's room.

Each of the four beds in Room 4-206 was occupied by an elderly lady. Grandmother Weird was in the bed closest to the door and Angie's stumble concluded at the foot of it. She looked her grandmother over. Her cheeks were rosy. Her eyes were bright. No tubes were attached to her, not even an intravenous line. In no way did Grandmother Weird appear to be on her deathbed.

"That's an awful lot of text," said a male voice. It came from the speaker in the telephone.

"Then make the letters small," Grandmother Weird said. She rolled her eyes. She saw Angie. She looked back at the telephone.

"No name? No date?" the speakerphone voice asked.

"Neither."

"It'll still be really small."

"I'll need it in thirteen days," Grandmother Weird said. She reached out her tiny arm. She jabbed her index finger to the telephone, ending the call. Shuffling her body back into the middle of the bed she looked her granddaughter over.

"Does it have a father?" Grandmother Weird asked.

"Are you asking if this is the child of God?"

"How far along?"

"They looked at me funny in the airport."

"But no ring . . ."

"Who am I to go against family tradition?" Angie asked. Grandmother Weird issued a small laugh. She hadn't been married when she'd given birth to her only son, Besnard, Angie's father. The laugh made Angie feel slightly safer. She attempted to sit on the corner of the bed. The mattress sagged. She slid off. She attempted this several more times. Then she noticed the chair in the corner. Pushing it towards the bed, Angie sat down.

"Are you done?"

"Yes."

"No more wiggling?"

"Nope."

"Okay then," Grandmother said. She smoothed the wrinkles from the sheet. "I'm dying."

"Again?"

"I will die at 7:39 p.m. on April 20. Not a second later or a moment earlier."

"Who doesn't love a countdown?"

"Thirteen days from today."

"Is there something special about that day?"

"It's my birthday. I guess it slipped your memory?"

"Death's not much of a party."

"I've asked you to come here because there are mistakes I've made. Mistakes I need your help correcting."

"I plan on living until I'm at least a hundred. Maybe older."

"Be quiet, Angelika!"

Grandmother Weird said these words in what Angie and her siblings called *the Tone.* They each had a pet theory to explain why it was so effective. Kent's was that her voice became all bass. Abba thought it was the way she stressed each word, making them all sound capitalized. Lucy's explanation was that her lung capacity allowed her to push out twice as much air; therefore her words came out twice as strongly. Angie liked all of these, but she felt that only Richard had gotten it right. His explanation was that she stripped all emotion from her voice, leaving only her harsh judgment.

However it worked, it made Angie comply. She sat still. She folded her hands in her lap. Grandmother Weird didn't speak and more than a minute passed.

"You've always been impatient," Grandmother Weird finally said. "Do you know that you were born in a hallway?"

"How could I forget?"

"You almost died in that hallway."

"Yup."

"With the cord wrapped so tight around your little throat."

"Crazy," Angie said. She'd stopped paying attention to her grandmother. The thought of giving birth in a hallway was so terrifying that she'd begun conjuring the scene in her mind, replaying it over and over. This was the way Angie often dealt with events she feared would happen.

"That's why I gave it to you," Grandmother Weird said.

"Of course."

"The power to forgive."

"I know. Wait. Gave me what?"

"It was your father's fault. That idiotic car. Whoever heard of driving a Maserati in the city? I knew it would define you."

"The car?"

"I knew you'd spend your whole life having to find it in yourself to forgive your parents for almost killing you before you were even born. With your very first breath you needed the power to forgive. It's odd because forgiveness is not something I'm particularly good at. I didn't even know I had it in me."

"What are we talking about?"

"The ability to forgive!"

" . . . "

"It's my heart," Grandmother Weird said. "My goddamn elephant heart."

Grandmother Weird's heart, while much smaller than an elephant's, *was* unnaturally large. The average human heart weighs between 250 and 350 grams and is about the size of a fist. The weight of Annie Weird's heart pushed 600 grams and it was the size of two fists together. She was convinced that its exaggerated dimensions were the source of all the drama that had ever befallen her. And she was well aware that Angie was her only grandchild who'd inherited this condition. Angie's heart was even slightly bigger than her own.

"I held you in my arms," Grandmother Weird continued. "I looked down and it came from me and tumbled into you. I gave to you the power to forgive anyone, anytime."

Angie looked down at Grandmother Weird. She saw how loosely her rings fit on her fingers, the tremor in her right hand and the droop in her eyelids. "That's so . . . it's . . . it's r . . . really b . . . eautiful," Angie said. She'd started to cry.

"Maybe I should have given you the power not to be such a crybaby sap," Grandmother Weird said.

Angie had a deserved reputation as the family's crybaby. Yet her grandmother's comment stung. "Couldn't it have been invisibility?" Angie asked, her tears ceasing, instantly. "Flight maybe? Something a little more useful?"

"You came out bright red. Not very attractive, I'm afraid. Like a boiled lobster!"

"Super-speed?"

"All of you got one, you know. All five of you got one."

"You gave Kent the power to be an asshole?"

"Yes. In a way I did. Kent is slightly stronger than anyone he fights. Physical fights, I mean. He came out so small and I knew he'd need to defend himself, somehow. That he's emotionally stunted is not my fault."

"He's not stunted. He's just angry all the time."

"Lucy is never lost. Abba never loses hope. Richard keeps

himself safe. I never thought they'd all become curses. They were supposed to be blessings. I didn't know that they'd end up ruining your lives."

"Our lives are ruined?"

"And it's not just you kids. It's the family. The family name! I will not go to the grave responsible for taking down the good name of the Weirds."

"Oh yes. Well, then, that makes more sense."

"That's why you're here, Angie. You must go and find them. Round all of them up and bring them here. All five of you must be in this room at 7:39 p.m. on April 20 precisely. At the moment of my death I will lift the curses."

"Can't you just lift mine now? If it's a curse, the sooner the better, no?"

"Again with the sass! Angie, I have no control over these things. I didn't consciously bestow these abilities. I can't consciously remove them. I just know that at the moment of my death, when my heart is confronted with a now or never situation, it will see the damage these curses have inflicted and take them away."

"I see," Angie said. She looked down at her belly. She put both of her hands on the arms of her chair and stood. A blue plastic pitcher sat beside the phone on the bedside table. She filled a Styrofoam cup with water and took a drink.

"Did you hear me?" Grandmother Weird asked.

"Even the water smells like pine."

"Look at me."

"Hmmm?"

"You think I've lost my mind."

"No. Not at all. It's just big. Big news. I just need some time to absorb it, that's all."

"I see. Perhaps a demonstration then?"

"Not necessary."

"There's a marker in there," Grandmother Weird said, pointing to the drawer in the bedside table. "Could you get it for me?"

Angie opened the drawer. She searched through it. Beneath several celebrity gossip magazines Angie found a black felt-tipped Magic Marker. She handed it over to her. Grandmother Weird took the cap off with her teeth and spit it out, sending it sailing through the air.

The instant the cap hit the floor, every light in the room dimmed by half. The television sets lost reception. Angie felt her grandmother's cold, bony fingers encircle her wrist. She tried to pull away but the old woman's grip was incredibly strong and she could not break it.

"Watch the little old ladies," Grandmother said.

Angie looked up. The elderly woman closest to the window fell backwards, as if she'd been deboned. The machine beside that bed made a high-pitched whine. Grandmother Weird pressed the Magic Marker against the skin of Angie's forearm and began to write. The lights dimmed further. The white-haired woman in the next bed collapsed. A second machine began making the high-pitched whine. A nurse ran into the room. Angie tried again to pry her grandmother's fingers away. She still couldn't. Grandmother Weird wrote a series of numbers on Angie's skin. The lady in the bed closest fell backwards. A third machine whined. More nurses ran into the room.

"Stop it!" Angie yelled. "Stop this right now!"

Her grandmother did not look up. She wrote the last number of a ten-digit sequence. Then she let go of Angie's wrist. The lights returned to full-strength. The televisions regained reception. The machines stopped making their high-pitched whines. The elderly women sat upright in their beds and looked around the room, dazed and frightened.

"Never doubt your elders, child."

"Shark!" Angie yelled. She began to back out of Room 4-206. "You will never hold my baby. You will never see me again."

"Yes I will," Grandmother Weird said. She smiled broadly. She began to laugh. She laughed in *the Tone*.

Angie backed out into the hallway. Holding her belly she ran as fast as she could. She did not look back. By the time she'd reached the elevators, Angie had already forgiven her grandmother.

Ninety minutes after fleeing her grandmother's hospital room Angie was scrubbing her forearm at a sink in the women's washroom on the departures level of the Vancouver International Airport. She'd rebooked her flight from the back of the taxi she'd taken from the hospital. The only other woman in the bathroom stood at the hand dryer. Her pantsuit was unwrinkled. The diamonds in her ears shone. She pretended not to stare at Angie. Then the dryer shut off and she gave Angie a gentle look as she walked confidently away on her strappy high heels.

Angie looked in the mirror. The front of her white blouse was soaked. Her belly button bulged through the cotton. The ten-digit number remained perfectly legible on her red forearm. When she heard the final boarding call for flight AC117 from Vancouver to New York City, Angie turned off the tap, headed to the gate and boarded the plane.

At row 18 a large man was sitting in the aisle seat. A third of him spilt over the chair. His right arm had already claimed the middle armrest. He did not look up as Angie pushed her purse into the overhead compartment. She stood for several moments before he moved into the aisle and then she wedged herself into the window seat.

Her revenge was how often she had to pee.

Angie made her first trip to the bathroom shortly after takeoff. Her second was twenty minutes later. When she returned from her third visit, the large man had moved to the window.

"Touché," he said as Angie lowered herself into the aisle seat.

"Thank you," she replied.

An hour and forty minutes later Angie was in the washroom for the sixth time when the plane began to plummet. She grabbed the faucet with her left hand, cradled her belly with her right and pushed her bum against the door. Water splashed onto the front of her shirt, soaking it once more. She immediately realized that Veronica was a stupid, stupid name. She made a promise to both God and her unborn daughter to find a better one, should they survive.

The dive lasted three long seconds. When the plane levelled off Angie ran back to her seat. She fastened her seat belt, tightly. The large man beside her opened the plastic window shade. They both squinted. When their eyes had adjusted to the light they saw thick black smoke billowing from the plane's far right engine.

"I wouldn't worry. There are three others," the man sitting beside her said. Then he wiggled into his chair, folded his hands over his chest and closed his eyes.

"Good afternoon," said an authoritative voice from the speaker over top of Angie's head. "This is your captain. Yes. We're experiencing some . . . minor . . . technical difficulties. Nothing to worry about, folks. But we're going to have to make an unscheduled stop. We should be landing in the . . . at the . . . Winnipeg James Armstrong Richardson International Airport in about fifteen, seventeen minutes. We . . . ah . . . apologize for the inconvenience. We'll be all right."

It was the *we'll be all right* that started the panic. There was a collective gasp. Angie's breathing became shallow. Superstition took over and she began to believe that if she could just decide on the perfect name they really would be *all right*. Sarah, Rachael, Jenny, Candi, she thought, desperately. "Vanessa, Abigail, Helen, Franny," she said out loud. Then the pressure overwhelmed her imagination and all she could come up with were random nouns. "Celery, Oboe, Loofah," she muttered. "Garamond, Decanter, Frizzante, Pilates. Rolex, Evian, Dasani, Perriella."

The plane began its descent, which was steep. It dipped forwards. It wobbled to the left and the right. Angie used both of her hands to clutch the armrest as she became convinced that they were all going to die a horrible fiery death.

Then she looked at her forearm and she instantly knew

what had to be done. Unfastening her seat belt Angie stepped into the aisle.

"Sit down!" yelled a flight attendant.

"I'm saving us all!" Angie yelled back.

The overhead compartment squeaked as Angie opened it. Pushing back a suitcase that started to fall out, she grabbed her purse, sat back down and fished her phone out. Then Angie dialed the number that she hadn't been able to wash away.

The plane jumped. The phone on the other end began to ring. The runway came into view. "Hold my hand!" she said to the man beside her. He opened his eyes and looked at Angie, blankly. "I'm pregnant and alone and frightened and you will hold my goddamn hand!"

Angie held her hand out. Her seatmate took it. He squeezed, tightly. The phone rang for a fourth time. The plane tilted to the right. Several passengers screamed. The phone rang again and then it was answered.

"I'll do it!" Angie yelled. "I'll get them. I'll get all of them. I'll bring them to you!"

The back tires hit the runway. The plane slowed. The front wheels touched down and the passengers applauded. Angie breathed out. She realized how tightly she was holding both the phone and the hand of the man in the seat beside her.

"I knew you'd come around," Grandmother Weird said.

"Wait. Wait, wait, wait. Before we commit to anything . . ."

"I'd start with Lucy."

"Well," Angie said. She looked out the window and then she looked at her hand, which was still engulfed by the meaty palm of her seatmate, "I *am* in Winnipeg."

ANGIE WEIRD REALLY WAS BORN in a hallway, and this is how it happened. On May 4, 1987, when her mother, Nicola, went into labour her father, Besnard, drove them to the hospital in his beloved 1947 maroon Maserati. Besnard had purchased the two-seater seventy-two hours before Angie's birth. It wasn't suited for city driving. Besnard wasn't used to driving it. He stalled six times on the way to the hospital.

His sixth stall happened at the southeast corner of College and University in downtown Toronto. They were close enough to the hospital that Nicola could see it. She sat in the passenger seat, staring at it longingly. She stared at Mount Sinai Hospital in a way she hadn't stared at her husband in quite some time.

Besnard sat in the driver's seat, trying to restart the engine. The car behind him began to honk. He sighed, deeply. The impending birth of his fourth child failed to excite him. He'd begun to see his children as some kind of venereal disease, direct results of copulation. At home he already had three children, all under the age of five. He loved all of them. He knew he would love this child too. This was the problem. As he continued trying to restart the engine, his wife opened the passenger door.

Nicola got out of the Maserati and walked the last two hundred yards on her own. The doors to emergency slid open automatically. The admitting nurse dropped her paperwork and rushed over. Nicola was put on a gurney and wheeled through the swinging doors before Besnard had a chance to park. Nicola screamed as she felt Angie's head start to crown. It was her fourth birthing experience and she knew that the worst was, or at least soon would be, over. They had almost reached the delivery room when a doctor ran up and stopped the gurney, examining Nicola right in the corridor.

"Do not push anymore! Stop!" he said.

"What are you talking about?" Nicola yelled.

"Stop pushing right now!" the doctor said, firmly. He looked into her eyes and held her hand, gestures that Nicola never forgot. She stopped pushing. She breathed as deeply as she could. She concentrated on these things, which is why she didn't notice how quiet everyone had become.

"Can I push now?"

"You cannot," the doctor replied. "The cord's around the baby's neck."

Nicola gritted her teeth. She did not push. So much pressure built up inside her that her nose started to bleed.

"Almost got it," the doctor said.

"My *goddamn* head is going to *goddamn* explode!"

"Got it!"

"Now?"

"Now!"

The cord unwound, Nicola pushed and Angelika Weird, quite literally, popped into the world.

Angie never doubted that any part of this story was true. The question she asked herself was: did it really have the deep character-forming significance that her grandmother claimed it had? Angie didn't believe it had any greater impact on her personality than the fact that she was born in early May, making her a Taurus. She would, however, admit that she had never been able to wear necklaces or turtlenecks. Nor had she ever been able to make herself do up the top button on any shirt.

It was with a nosebleed that Grandmother Weird got herself admitted into Vancouver and District General Hospital, eight days before she wrote her phone number on Angie's forearm. She finished her lunch and washed her dishes and then she took a taxi to the emergency room. It was 2:30 p.m. when she stepped into the line. Fifteen minutes later, when she got to the front of it, Annie told the triage nurse that she was terminally ill.

"Could you be more specific?" the nurse asked.

"My death will occur at 7:39 p.m. on April 20."

"That is *very* specific."

"Twenty-one days from today."

"Maybe you could come back on the nineteenth?"

"Maybe you should watch your tone."

"Maybe *you* should take a seat."

The nurse looked down at her paperwork. She did not look back up. Annie took a seat beside a woman whose skin had taken on a yellowish hue. She folded her hands in her lap. She stared straight ahead. She set herself an impossible task: she would not move until her name was called.

A parade of broken limbs, troubling coughs and exaggerated parental fears came and went. Just after 4:30 in the morning, after sitting still for fourteen hours, Annie was alone in the waiting room for the first time.

"Angela Weirs?" a nurse called.

"Close enough," Annie said. She stood. Her joints were stiff. She took small jerky steps. The nurse led her into a room with curtains for walls. The thin brown paper crinkled as Annie sat on it. Her feet were a long way from the floor. She swung them. She waited for quite some time and then a doctor arrived. He was yawning, stubbled, and a third her age.

"So. You are dying?" he asked. He looked at her and then down at his clipboard. "Slowly."

The doctor put in the earpieces of his stethoscope. He placed the chestpiece on Annie's chest. He listened to her heart. He took the instrument off her skin and blew into it. Then he put it back on her chest and listened again.

"That is the loudest heartbeat I've ever heard."

"I have a very large heart."

"It does, however, sound like it's working perfectly."

"I'm not here because I'm sick."

"Okay. Then why are you here?"

"It is imperative that I stay alive until 7:39 p.m. on April 20."

"Well, you see, that's a problem," the doctor said. He gave a small laugh and then he sat down beside her. "That's not really what we do here. We help sick people get better and you, I guess unfortunately, aren't exhibiting any symptoms."

"What sort of things are you looking for?"

"Difficulty breathing? Dizziness? Sustained aches and pains. Loss of consciousness. You know, things like that. We work best with symptoms."

"Bleeding nose?"

"That would be a start," he said. He signed the bottom of the page. When he looked back up he saw thin but strengthening lines of blood running from both of Annie's nostrils. As her eyes rolled back in her head the doctor rushed to catch her.

AT THE EXACT MOMENT THE WHEELS of Angie's plane touched the runway, Lucy Weird, the second oldest, straddled a stranger on the second floor of the Millennium Library in Winnipeg. She was in the stacks, by the 813s. It was the library's least frequented area. Lucy's shirt was buttoned to the top. Her grey wool skirt fanned out in a circle. The library patron lay on the floor, on his back, wearing nothing.

Lucy slid down. She waited for the sound of his voice.

"Forty-nine," he said. Lucy pushed up. She slid back down. "Forty-eight," he said.

Lucy took a deep breath. She repeated the cycle. She closed her eyes. Her eyes remained closed as Beth, her least favourite co-worker, pushed a book cart towards the 800s. Beth looked up and took in the scene. Leaving the book cart behind, she scurried away.

Unaware, Lucy continued. "Twenty-six," the man beneath her said. Lucy focused on keeping a steady, yet building, rhythm. It wasn't long before she heard footsteps. The footsteps came closer. When the footsteps stopped, so did she.

Lucy leaned backwards and put her hand over the young man's mouth. She kept her eyes closed.

"Amanda?" Lucy asked.

"Yes. It's me."

"And who? There's someone else. Is it Beth?"

"Hello."

"At least I've made someone happy today."

"Woo mmad meee haappi," the man underneath Lucy said. She pushed her hand down harder.

"This is very bad, Lucy," Amanda said.

"Fired bad?"

"Help your friend get dressed and then come to the office."

"Okay," Lucy said. She nodded her head. She kept her eyes closed. She listened to the footsteps walk away. When she couldn't hear them anymore Lucy took her hand off the man's mouth. She leaned forwards. "Start again," Lucy whispered.

"What?"

"From the top!" Lucy said.

"Two hundred and eighty-seven," he said. Lucy pushed up and then she slid back down. "Two hundred and eighty six," he said.

"One!" the young man said.

Lucy breathed deeply in. For several blissful moments sensation overwhelmed her. She felt that everything was beyond her control. She felt free and limitless, almost lost. Then it all went away. Lucy stood up. She adjusted her clothes. She picked up his shirt and held it by the shoulders as he put his arms through the sleeves.

"I want to see you again," he said.

"Close your eyes," Lucy said. He closed his eyes. She bent down and picked up his boxer briefs. "Now open them."

"Okay?"

"There! You've done it. You've seen me again!" Lucy said and she handed him his underwear.

Without looking back Lucy walked out of the stacks. She went to the bathroom. Then she went into Amanda's office, which was small, windowless and cluttered. There was a stack of files on the corner of her desk. It leaned to the left. Lucy looked at the floor. She looked at the far wall. She clasped her hands behind her back. Then she grabbed the pile, turned all of it sideways and tapped it against the desk until every folder was perfectly aligned.

"You need help," Amanda said.

"I don't deny it," Lucy said. She set the pile back on the corner of Amanda's desk.

"And what's with the hair?"

"I just got it cut," Lucy said. She tucked the right side of her bangs behind her ear. There was nothing she could do about the three tufts that stuck up at the back.

"It's just so clichéd, Lucy."

"You mean the naughty librarian thing?"

"Don't even say that. This is the first time that anything like this has ever happened here."

"It's the first time you've caught me."

"You're fired."

"Usually I'm pretty safe up there in North American Literature."

"Collect your things and go."

Lucy extended her index finger and adjusted the files, slightly. She nodded her head. She left Amanda's office. There was nothing she needed to collect from her desk and no co-workers she needed to say good-bye to. Lucy walked to the main doors and went through them.

On the sidewalk Lucy stood perfectly still. Having just been fired in a ridiculous and humiliating way, she wanted to feel shame, to be so overwhelmed by self-doubt that she no longer knew who she was. She wanted to feel lost. But all she felt was the dry dusty air. A bus stopped in front of her. She hadn't realized that she had been standing at a bus stop, but when the doors opened Lucy decided to get on.

There were twelve people on the bus. Lucy counted each one as she walked by them. She took a seat at the very back. She closed her eyes. The bus rounded many corners. Her body shifted and swayed. When she was sure that she'd lost track of time, Lucy pulled the cord.

Lucy stepped off of the bus. She watched it drive away. Then she looked around. The houses were mainly sixties-era bungalows. The lawns were perfectly kept. The street signs told her that she stood at Druid and Forester. Lucy had never been here. She had never heard of either of these streets. She wasn't even sure what part of town she was in. But Lucy knew, without doubt, that if she went six blocks north, and then four blocks west, and then south for another nine and a half blocks, she'd be in front of her house.

"Damn it!" Lucy said.

She walked into the middle of the road. She closed her eyes and she held out her arms and she turned in a slow clockwise circle. But no matter what direction Lucy faced, she knew the way home.

ANGIE SET THE TIMER ON HER PHONE and waited on the sidewalk across from her sister's house. Forty-five minutes passed before a dented and dirty taxi arrived and Lucy stepped out of it. It had been nearly eight years since Angie had seen her sister and the first thing she noticed, and then couldn't stop staring at, was her haircut. The bangs on the right side of Lucy's head were at least three inches longer than the bangs on the left. The bottom was sliced in a zig-zag, like the mouth of a jack-o'-lantern. Three tufts stuck up at the top. Lucy's haircut didn't look fashionable or avant-garde—it just looked crazy.

Angie walked across the street. Lucy turned and saw her coming. They stopped when they were three feet apart. Neither decreased the space between them. Angie tried not to stare at Lucy's hair.

"It's me. Your sister. Angie."

"I didn't know you were coming."

"I didn't either."

"Your boobs are so big!"

"Well, I *am* pregnant."

"How did you find my house?"

"You're in the phone book."

"Right."

"Do you want to know how long I waited?"

"Yes!"

Angie took her phone out of her purse. She checked the timer. "Forty-seven minutes," she said. "And twenty seconds from right . . . now."

"That's not so bad."

"No. I guess it isn't."

"Can you give me five minutes?"

"Of course," Angie said, setting the timer again. Lucy turned. She ran up the steps to her house. Her hair was just as ragged in the back.

Angie had always known her sister to be tightly wound. Lucy had obsessed over her grades. She was considered one of the prettiest girls in her school, yet she never went out with anyone. At the same time she was a bit of a slut, although her choice of partners had always seemed more than literally beneath her. Growing up Lucy had always disliked surprises. As Angie stood on the sidewalk in front of her house, she assumed that her sister's desire for control had finally broken her.

Angie's timer dinged. She walked across the front lawn, which was manicured to a golf-green perfection. Picking the blades of grass off her shoes Angie knocked on the door. It was immediately answered.

"Angie!" Lucy called.

"May I come in?"

"Please do," Lucy said, and Angie stepped inside.

Two skinny floor rugs lay side by side in the hallway. Angie stood by the door. She could see into the living room, where matching white armchairs were pushed against the far wall. Both rooms were without coffee mugs or newspapers or anything accidental. It did not look like anyone lived there. It looked like an advertisement.

"Can you take your shoes off?" Lucy asked.

"Um . . ."

"Please."

"Give me a minute," Angie said. She sat on the floor and lifted her feet into the air.

"Come on, Angie, you're a big girl now."

"Obviously you've never been pregnant."

"It's not too late," Lucy said. She crossed her arms. Angie kept her feet in the air. The effort strained her stomach muscles.

"If you want them off you'll have to do it," Angie said.

"So, what? You never take your shoes off?"

"It's just hard."

"You sleep in those shoes?"

"You can't just help me out here?"

"Not if you can't help yourself!"

"Fine," Angie yelled. She wedged off her left shoe with her right foot. It flew into the air and landed upside down on the left rug. She did the same with the other shoe, which landed on the right rug. Lucy collected both shoes. She set them inside the hall closet, next to her own. Then she reached out her hand and helped Angie to her feet.

"The hard part is getting them back on."

"Well, maybe I can help you with that," Lucy said.

The two sisters walked into the living room. Lucy sat in the left armchair. Angie lowered herself into the other one. She watched her sister, knowing that Lucy would be trying to predict what she was about to say. Angie waited some moments. She waited a few more. Then she just came out with it.

"I went to see the Shark!" Angie said. This was the name the Weird siblings routinely used when referring to their grandmother.

"Good God why?"

"Didn't expect that, did you?"

"No. I did not."

"She says that she's on her deathbed."

"Again?"

"I know, I know."

"Is she still on Blake Street?"

"No. She's in the hospital. Vancouver and District. Room 4-206."

"Do tell."

"Don't get excited. She doesn't seem sick at all. She does however claim that she will die on her birthday."

"Very dramatic."

"She was pretty convincing, Lucy."

"You're the only one who still falls for the bleeding nose thing."

"She also claims—"

"It's not as if we all couldn't do it. So handy for getting out of phys. ed., remember?"

"She also claims that she gave us all special powers when we were born."

"Beautiful."

"At the time she thought they were blessings. But now she realizes that they were curses."

"Blursings!"

"Let me finish—"

"What did you get?"

"Listen to me!"

"What does she claim to have given you?"

"I can always forgive."

"And me?"

"You're never lost."

"She always liked you better."

"Luce! Listen! I believe her!"

"Oh you do not."

"I'm starting to," Angie said. She looked up at her sister. She wished everything didn't always have to be so hard. "Ask yourself. Have you ever been lost?"

"I have a natural sense of direction."

"Exactly. And I've let almost everybody I've ever met walk all over me."

"That's not just low self-esteem?"

"She's charged me with collecting all of us and bringing everyone to her hospital room so that at the moment of her death she can lift the curses."

"She gave you—a quest?"

"Don't mock me."

"Don't be mockable."

"Thirteen days . . ."

"You're really taking this seriously?"

"It seemed like a lot of time but now it doesn't."

"Does anyone know where Kent is?"

"That seems like enough time? Right?" Angie asked. She looked at her sister and saw a mixture of pity and skepticism. "You think I've gone crazy."

"No. No. It's just big. That's all. A lot to take in."

"There were ladies falling unconscious and nurses rushing in and then the lights dimmed. She grabbed my arm and she wrote her phone number on it and I still can't wash it off. Our plane was on fire! We had to make an emergency landing. We were all going to die! And then I called the number! I agreed to do it! Then the plane landed safely!"

"Do you want some tea? I have the kettle on."

"Are you hearing this?"

"Do you really believe that the plane would have crashed

if you hadn't called the Shark?"

"I think . . . yes, I do."

"Angie, that's called magical thinking. You've always been prone to it. The whole family has. It's okay, but it's a certifiable mental illness. It's in all the textbooks."

"You think it's just a coincidence that we were forced to land in Winnipeg?"

"I think it even has its own drug now," Lucy said.

Neither sister said anything more. Angie swallowed several times. She bit the inside of her cheek. She tried to take deep breaths. But none of it worked. The tears came. Angie started to sob.

"I'm not going to do it just because you're crying."

"I'm s . . . s . . . sorry. I'm not trying t . . . oo. I'm trying rea . . . lly hard n . . . ot to," Angie said. She wiped her nose with her sleeve. Slightly revolted, Lucy retrieved a box of Kleenex, which she handed to her sister. Angie blew her nose but her chest still heaved.

"I lost my job today," Lucy said. "I got caught fucking a stranger in front of the 813s."

"No w . . . ay!"

"I did."

"Just like . . . when you . . . worked at F . . . f . . . rosty Queen?"

"Yes."

"And . . . at . . . I . . . deal Coffee . . . and Cinnamon . . . To . . . Go?"

"No need to make a list."

"But don't you . . . th . . . ink . . . that's too . . . coinci . . . dental? You getting fired . . . today?"

"It doesn't mean anything, Angie."

"Okay," Angie said. She blew her nose again. She took several deep breaths but then she started sobbing again.

"Oh Jesus Christ," Lucy said. "I'll go see Abba."

"Really? You . . . will?"

"Only because we should have done it a long time ago."

"Thank you, Lucy. That . . . means . . . so . . . m . . . uch."

"I can't believe that still works."

"It's . . . because . . . you have . . . a good . . . heart."

"Too bad for me."

"But y . . . ou'll really . . . go?"

"Yes, yes. I just said I would. I'll go as far as Abba," Lucy said. Angie nodded. She pushed herself out of the white armchair and moved across the room, lowering herself onto Lucy's chair, sitting half beside her sister and half on top of her. She turned herself sideways so she could hug Lucy.

"Watch my shirt."

"This . . . means . . . so . . . much . . . to . . . me."

"Careful with your nose. Here, blow. Everything's going to be okay. There's just one thing we'll have to do first."

"What is it?"

"We have to visit Mother."

"Okay," Angie said. "I'll do it."

In the kitchen the kettle began to whistle. This was a trick

Lucy had been using since high school, to interrupt moments precisely like this one. It got louder and louder and higher in pitch. But Angie didn't loosen her grip and Lucy did not try to break it.

THE MOST IMPORTANT THING the Weird siblings ever did together was Rainytown. It was a city made entirely out of cardboard boxes that they built in the half-storey attic of their family's cottage. It was a project they worked on every summer, whenever it rained. Two factors contributed significantly to its genesis: that it rained for seven straight days during the summer of 1994, and that several weeks earlier Kent had found numerous cardboard boxes, big and small, in a neighbour's garbage.

Kent had dragged the boxes back to the cottage with the intention of playing girlbots. This was a game that Lucy and Abba were disinclined to join. It was forgotten until the grey dismal morning of the seventh day, when they looked outside and saw that the rain continued to fall. Lacking fresh ideas, they followed Kent up to the attic, where conflict began almost instantly.

"Hold on there, Kentucky," Richard said, using the nickname he knew Kent hated. "I'm obviously the mad scientist since I can't be a girlbot and I'm older than you."

"That's not fair!" Kent said. A small trickle of blood began to leak from his left nostril.

"Truth isn't fair," Richard said, invoking the expression that was the unofficial Weird family motto.

"You know that isn't going to work with us," Abba said. Kent's nosebleed ceased.

"Just because I'm a girl doesn't mean I can't be the mad scientist," Lucy said. She began collecting boxes. Richard tried to pull them out of her hands. Fighting ensued. Their voices rose in volume and pitch and soon their mother's head poked up into the crawl space.

What she saw disturbed her. Abba appeared to be crying, although it was hard to tell because of the box that covered her head. Angie was also in tears—but then again when wasn't she?—because she couldn't remove the Kleenex boxes that had been duct-taped to her feet. Lucy repeatedly hit Richard on the head with a long cardboard tube.

"Stop it," their mother screamed. "Stop it! Stop it! Stop it!"

Nicola, who was not prone to losing it, looked at her children. She looked at the boxes scattered on the floor. "What are you people trying to do?" she asked.

"Make robots," Kent truthfully answered.

"Robots? Surely the five of you can come up with something better than that. Something more . . ."

A silence followed. The sound of the rain striking the roof could be heard. Their mother's eyes seemed to be focused on something quite far away. The silence captured their attention, and the look on Nicola's face, wistful and sad, cracked their self-absorbed shells.

"More what?"

"Just more. Larger. A bigger scale," Nicola said. "Not a mimic of some movie. Something original. Something that can be all your own . . ."

"Okay . . ."

"But like what?"

"What, Mom? Tell us!"

"Like a city!"

"That's a great idea!"

"From Mom!"

"Why so surprised?"

"How should we start?"

"A town hall?"

"A TV station!"

"A motorcycle speedway!"

"You choose, Mom," Richard said. "What would you start with?"

"A hair salon," she said, instantly. "A beauty parlour."

And so they got started. That very afternoon they designed and built the It's About Time Hair Cutting Saloon, situated in what would become the heart of Rainytown, the first of many buildings to follow.

If it hadn't been for Besnard there were many things Nicola would have done with her life. But after he vanished she didn't do any of them. She didn't even try. Two days after her husband's crumpled Maserati was pulled from Georgian Bay, having apparently veered off the road and over a cliff, Nicola went into her bedroom. She closed the door. She did not come out.

The Weird siblings assumed that their mother was waiting for their father's body to be found, just like they were. When the Maserati was towed out of the water, Besnard's body had not come with it. It was thought that it had been swept away by the tide and that the same forces would soon push it back to shore. But two weeks later their father's body had not been found and their mother had not come out of her room.

The meals she placed in the hallway went untouched, and Angie began to suspect that her mother was leaving the bedroom at night and making her own food. Angie set her alarm for 3:30 a.m. She crept downstairs, to the kitchen. To keep herself awake she brewed a pot of coffee. This was the first time she'd ever tried to do this. Angie took one sip and dumped the rest into the sink; it was the last coffee she ever tasted.

Angie sat at the kitchen table and waited. Without anything to keep her awake, she soon fell asleep. When she woke up her mother stood at the counter. Nicola wore a black pantsuit, heels and a small string of pearls. She was making a loaf of sandwiches. Angie watched her butter twelve slices of bread. She set down the knife and opened the refrigerator.

The light from inside shone on her carefully styled hair. She took out a jar of pickles and strained to open it.

"At least I know you're eating," Angie said. Her mother didn't seem to hear her. She continued trying to open the pickle jar. "I said, it's good to know that you're eating!"

Frustrated, Nicola set the unopened jar on the counter. Angie went over to the cutlery drawer. She took out a knife and tapped the lid of the pickle jar in a circle. Then she set the jar back on the counter and put the knife back in the drawer. As she returned to her seat at the table, Nicola made another attempt to open the jar.

"Hey? Mom?"

"Yes!" Nicola said as the lid popped open. She fished out four pickles, sliced them and put them on the buttered bread. She got a tomato from the refrigerator. Angie took it off the counter. She held it in her hand. Her mother went back to the refrigerator and took another tomato out of the crisper.

"Please don't do this," Angie said. "Don't do this to us."

Nicola sliced the tomato. She put her pieces of bread together, stacked all the sandwiches on a dinner plate and carried the stack towards the kitchen doorway. Angie got up and stood in front of her mother. Nicola stopped. The sandwiches wobbled. For the briefest moment Angie was sure that her mother recognized her and that everything was going to be okay. But then the look of recognition disappeared. It went away so quickly that Angie couldn't tell whether she'd caught her mother off guard and seen through her act, or if the look hadn't really been there in the first place. Keeping the plate level Nicola bent forwards at the waist. She leaned down until she and Angie were eye to eye.

"Are you staying here too? It's such a beautiful hotel," Nicola said.

Not being recognized by her mother was unsettling, yet what troubled Angie even more was how much confidence and joy there was in Nicola's voice. Emotions it had not conveyed for as long as Angie could remember.

"What's your name?" Nicola asked.

"Please. Mom? Don't?"

"Well, whoever you are," she said and she lifted her left hand, extended her index finger and dabbed Angie on the nose, "you're as cute as a bug!"

Angie looked at the floor. She watched her mother's shoes as they stepped around her. She did not turn around as Nicola Weird left the room and climbed the stairs and stopped being her mom forever.

ANGIE WAS SURPRISED WHEN Lucy handed her a pillow and a sheet. "Wait," she said. "I have to sleep on a couch and I have to make it up? This is no way to treat a guest."

"You're not a guest, you're family," Lucy said. Angie started to cry. Lucy turned out the light.

In the morning Angie woke up with stiff legs and a sore back. She took tiny steps into the kitchen, where Lucy had already made breakfast.

"Do you drink coffee yet?" Lucy asked. Angie shook her head no. Lucy poured her a glass of orange juice. The hard-boiled eggs were perfectly timed. The toast was golden. Their taxi arrived at 8:55. Lucy's suitcase was already at the door and Angie rushed to collect her things. Checking the lock three times, Lucy then carried both of their bags to the sidewalk. Here they stood for several moments as Angie inspected the cab.

In 1963 Angie's grandfather Samuel D. Weird founded the Grace Taxi Service. He named the enterprise after his mother. When Besnard took over the business, in 1982, it had grown into the second largest fleet in the city of Toronto.

Over time Besnard developed many theories about taxis. For one, he believed that you should make a wish while hailing a cab. If the first taxi that passed by stopped and picked you up, your wish would come true. He also felt that every taxi ride was metaphorical—that it could be interpreted, like tea leaves or the lines in your palm. But his most firmly held theory was that your choice of taxi was a reflection of how you saw yourself. Of all his theories, this was the one that had been most firmly passed on to his children.

"No visible dents or scratches," Angie said. She circled the cab slowly.

"You still do this?"

"I would have liked a newer model," Angie said as she came back around to the back passenger door.

"Not in this town."

"Really?"

"'Fraid so."

"Okay, let's take it," Angie said. She slid into the back seat. "To the airport," she told the driver.

"But first," Lucy said as she got into the back seat and closed the door, "the Golden Sunsets Retirement Community, 170 Lipton Street."

"I didn't think you meant right away," Angie said.

"Well, when did you think I meant?"

"I don't know. Soonish? You know. In the near future."

Lucy rolled her eyes. Six minutes later the cab stopped in front of 170 Lipton Street. The exterior of the Golden Sunsets Retirement Community was concrete and depressing. It was worse inside. Decades of wheelchairs had worn twin tracks into the thin grey carpet. The grandfather clock in the lobby leaned to the left. It smelled like medicine and the walls were painted a yellow that was much too optimistic.

"Is this really the best we can afford?" Angie asked.

"This is more than we can afford."

They walked down the corridor. Angie tried not to look into the rooms. She failed. Some of the residents met her eyes. Others just stared through her. But most disturbing to Angie were their haircuts—zigzag patterns and asymmetrical bobs and parts that started just above the ear. Every single resident there sported a hairdo that looked suspiciously like Lucy's.

"What's with the hair?" Angie asked.

"You'll see," Lucy said, and she pressed the down button. The elevator arrived and they stepped inside. Neither spoke. When the doors opened for B2, Lucy pointed to a handwritten cardboard sign masking-taped directly across the hall. The sign read:

IT'S ABOUT TIME HAIR CUTTING SALOON

Angie stepped out of the elevator. The doors began to close. "I'd go with you but I've just had mine done," Lucy said.

"This is for real?" Angie asked her.

"Don't worry," Lucy said. She held out her hand. The doors jumped back open. "She won't even recognize you."

Lucy removed her hand. The elevator closed. Angie took three steps forwards. She stood in front of the door that the sign was taped to. The handle was long and metal. Angie held it for several seconds. Then she pushed it down and went inside.

The room was obviously a disused janitor's closet. It was small and lit by a single floor lamp. A shelf made of two-by-fours and plywood covered the back wall. There was a sink in the corner. Several mops hung to the right of it. Across from the sink was a wooden kitchen chair on which her mother slept.

Angie watched her sleep. She counted to sixty in her head. She gave the door a good shove, and Nicola woke up.

"Can I help you?"

"It's me. Angie," she said. She watched Nicola carefully. For a fraction of a second Angie was sure that her mother recognized her. But the look quickly disappeared and, once again, Angie couldn't be sure if she'd caught her or imagined something that wasn't there.

"You're here for a haircut?"

"It's me. Your fourth born. Angie."

"You're in luck. Mr. Weston cancelled."

"I'm about to have a baby . . ."

"I guess I should say *he* was cancelled."

"Really? Nothing?"

"God rest his soul," Nicola said. She picked up the chair, turned it around and set it backwards in front of the sink. She patted it and Angie sat down. Her mother tied a peach-coloured beach towel around her neck. She touched Angie's forehead, gently encouraging her to tilt back her head. Nicola washed Angie's hair. The water was warm. The shampoo smelled like goat's milk soap, which made Angie remember bathtubs full of siblings in their house on Palmerston Boulevard. She drifted off to sleep. She woke up with wet hair.

"You must be tired."

"I didn't feel that tired."

"Something about this room just makes people wanna sleep," Nicola said. She pulled a white towel from the far wall, revealing a mirror. "Nothing worse than staring at yourself all day," she said.

Angie stood and Nicola moved the chair in front of the mirror. Angie sat down. She looked at her mother's reflection. Nicola gathered Angie's wet hair and let it fall over her shoulders.

"What were you thinking?"

"A trim?"

"I think it needs more than that."

"No. Oh no. You know? Just a trim."

"Why don't you let me try something?"

"A trim is all I need. Really."

Nicola nodded in agreement. She reached for her scissors, took a five-inch length of her daughter's hair between her fingers and with a firm unhesitating motion, cut. A length of black hair dropped to the floor. Angie stared at it. A second clump, even longer, fell beside it. In the mirror she saw a third length between the jaws of her mother's scissors and as they started to close, Angie shut her eyes.

"How far along are you?"

"Hmmm?"

"I know you're not supposed to ask, but I don't know who wouldn't know there's a baby in there."

"Thirty-five weeks. Ish?"

"A girl?"

"Yes, it is."

"I thought so. You're carrying pretty low for it to be a boy."

"If she'd been a boy I was going to name her Besnard."

"You're going it alone?"

"After my father. Besnard. Besnard Richard Weird?" Angie said. She opened her eyes. Nicola continued cutting.

"Sorry," she said. "No ring, that's all. Am I prying?"

"No. You're not. There isn't one."

Angie's mother made a clucking sound with her tongue.

"You disapprove?" Angie asked.

"If a woman wants a child there's nothing worse than not having one. It's just very hard to do it on your own."

"Do you have children?"

"No, no. Well, almost."

"What happened?"

"I lost my husband."

"How?"

"A storm."

"A storm?"

"The Great Storm of 2001. He was lost at sea. Do you remember it? That storm?" she asked. The scissors stopped. They looked at each other in the mirror.

"Of course."

"Were you in it?"

"Sometimes I feel like I still am."

"Did you lose someone too?"

"I did," Angie said. Nicola nodded. She resumed cutting Angie's hair. She made six more slices at the back. Then three quick stabs to the top. She held up a length from the right side of Angie's head and cut at what seemed to be a randomly chosen point. She did the same on the left side. Exchanging her scissors for the hair dryer, Nicola flicked it to the highest setting and only then did Angie let herself cry.

Nicola turned off the hair dryer and stepped away. Angie looked in the mirror. Her hair seemed even more chaotic than Lucy's. Some sections on the right side seemed untouched, while all the hair on the left was cut quite short. Her bangs had been sliced into a zigzag pattern. Four tufts stuck up from the top.

"So?" Nicola asked. "Do you like it?"

"I love it, Mom," Angie said. "It's perfect."

Lucy was waiting by the elevator. The expression on her face remained neutral. She pressed the up button but the elevator doors did not open and then she started to laugh.

"We could be twins!" Lucy said. She ran her hands all over Angie's head.

"It is really that bad?"

"I didn't think you'd actually go through with it."

"I still think she's faking."

"She's not faking."

"I saw a look. A look of recognition. Just for a moment," Angie said.

Lucy stopped. She took Angie's hands. She held them tightly and she did not loosen her grip. "She fakes that," Lucy said. "That she does fake, no doubt."

"She fakes what?"

"She pretends, just at first, just for a moment, that she recognizes you. Just to see if she's supposed to. Then it goes away. It always goes away."

There was a ping and the elevator doors opened and they stepped inside.

"I didn't think of that," Angie said.

"It always goes away."

"Still. Maybe. I don't know."

"Stop playing with it."

"How bad is it?"

"We have to get to the airport. Our plane leaves at 11:15."

"I really appreciate this . . ."

"It's no big deal. Don't cry."

"I'm not . . . crying."

"It's okay. Calm down. It'll all be all right."

"Everything's . . . so . . . e . . . motional . . . right . . . now."

"I know. I know it is," Lucy said, "as it always has been."

The elevator doors opened. They followed the wheelchair tracks to the lobby. The taxi was still waiting for them.

When Richard Weird woke up and looked at the clock beside his bed it was 11:56. He studied the pillow beside him. It did not appear to have been slept on and he knew that she was gone.

Richard lay on his back and looked at the ceiling. It had just been painted cloud white. His wife's absence provoked the same emotional response as the ceiling did. This made him feel shallow and flawed but also relieved. It made him feel safe.

Sitting on the edge of the bed Richard pushed his toes into the blue shag carpet. He took his cigarettes from the bedside table. He lit one. He inhaled deeply. It was halfway done when he stood up. The inch-long ash fell to the floor. Richard walked across the room and opened the top drawer of his dresser. Underneath his socks he found the purple bag with the yellow drawstring. He opened it and turned it upside down. Two wedding rings, and nothing else, fell out.

One of the rings was silver. It had been given to him by his first wife, Nancy Kensington. They were married in March of 2003, less than two years after the death of his father. Their union had lasted seventeen months. It ended primarily because he met Debra Campbell.

Debra gave Richard the other ring, which was gold, during a service conducted on August 5, 2005. This was the day his divorce from Nancy was finalized. From the moment they ran out of city hall and onto Queen Street, Richard felt himself drifting away. They stuck it out another ten months. Debra claimed that his emotional distance was a conscious decision and Richard had been unable to disagree.

He then, determinedly, stayed single for another three years. He married Sarah English, the woman who'd given him the ring that was still on his finger, on September 20, 2009. He married her believing that their love was forever. And every day Richard woke up beside his wife, he found himself a little more in love with her. This meant that every day he felt just a little more vulnerable to her. It was merely a consequence of time before, feeling increasingly unsafe, Richard began to pull away.

This had happened in all three of his marriages. It had happened with every woman he'd ever fallen in love with.

Richard switched the cigarette from his left hand to his right and put the knuckle of his ring finger in his mouth. Wetting the skin, he slid the ring off. He put it inside the purple bag. He put the two other rings back inside it as well. Then he drew the yellow drawstring and placed the bag underneath his socks. As he closed the drawer more ash fell to the carpet.

He was in the bathroom, midstream, when he noticed that something had been written in soap on the bathroom mirror. He flushed the toilet. He washed his hands. Then he read the message.

> Richard:
> I'm sorry but I'm leaving you.
> I think you want it this way. I
> think you still love me (OVER)

"Over?" Richard asked.

For several moments Richard looked at his reflection. The word *sorry* appeared to be written on his forehead. Then he opened the medicine cabinet. The writing, still in soap, continued on the inside of the door. The back of the medicine cabinet was white and so was the soap. Richard opened and closed the door until he found an angle that allowed him to read it.

> If you do, prove it. I am flying
> home. My plane leaves at 5:15.
> We have something worth
> keeping. Don't be afraid of me.
> Sarah

Richard shut the door of the medicine cabinet. The sun broke through the clouds, filling the bathroom with light.

Richard ran to the bedroom and took his camera from the bedside table. He returned to the bathroom. The light was still perfect. He took many pictures from many angles of the medicine cabinet and the note that was written on the mirror. Only when the light faded did he lower his camera. Then he went back to the bedroom, dressed, took his wedding ring out of the bag and put it back on his finger. He packed a suitcase and called for an airport limo.

When the limo arrived Richard inspected it and found it met his approval.

Richard arrived at the Montréal-Pierre Elliott Trudeau International Airport just before four. A ticket for American Airlines flight AA487 to Washington, D.C. was easily purchased. He checked his bag. He stood in the line to enter security screening. It was 4:25. The security guard held out his hand for Richard's boarding pass. Richard reached into his pocket. He touched it. But the paper felt cold. He did not feel that it would keep him safe. Richard took his hand out of his pocket, leaving the boarding pass inside.

"Est-ce que je peux vous aider?" the guard asked.

"No, I don't think you can," Richard replied. He picked up his suitcase, stepped out of line and walked away. He was almost out of the airport, so close to the automatic doors that they'd rumbled open, when he saw them. He reached out and touched them. Angie and Lucy turned around and Richard, who had already raised his camera, took a picture.

WHEN NICOLA WENT INTO LABOUR with Richard, she was not surprised that her husband put her into the back of a taxi, or that he got behind the wheel, but that he started the meter. It was March 16, 1982. Nicola sat in the back seat. She gripped the door handle as another contraction went through her. When she looked back up the amount owing on the meter equalled the number of months she'd been married—$3.00.

In those three months Nicola had been unable to determine whether she loved Besnard, or just the chaos that he brought into her life. But as their unplanned pregnancy continued on schedule, there had been less and less time to worry about this. And now that the baby was almost here, the question was irrelevant: if she loved him, fantastic; if she only loved the chaos, there seemed to be no shortage of it.

Besnard raced south on University. He sped past cars, aiming for pockets of space that hadn't yet opened up. Nicola held the door handle tighter. She found this thrilling. It was the first time she'd seen him behind the wheel. Besnard had been driving a cab for four months, learning the ropes of his father's business, the Grace Taxi Service, which he was set to inherit. As they approached College Street, Nicola felt another contraction starting and the car went faster.

The traffic light was yellow. The taxi increased its speed, again—Nicola tightened her grip. The light turned red. She closed her eyes. They sped forwards. She heard a metallic crunch and the back end of the taxi jumped to the left. But they didn't stop.

Nicola opened her eyes and saw Besnard correcting the skid. He slowed down. He looked in the rear-view mirror. Once he'd seen that the damage to the red Ford Falcon was minimal, he sped up again. Thirty seconds later he stopped in front of Mount Sinai Hospital. He turned off the meter.

"Seven dollars and twenty-five cents!" he said, "Unheard of!"

"You could have killed us!"

"But I didn't."

"That's true," Nicola said. She wanted to be angry but what she really felt was protected. That he would break so many laws to get her to the hospital as quickly as possible boded well, she felt. The delivery, although stunningly painful, was without complications and Besnard Richard Weird Jr. came into the world six hours later.

The following morning, Grandmother Weird arrived at 9:45 a.m., fifteen minutes before visiting hours began. She was about to turn fifty-four. Her son was only twenty-two. His bride a mere nineteen. As she took the infant into her arms, a sense of maternal responsibility swelled up inside her such as she had never felt before—not even with Besnard. It was at this exact moment that the child's parents began to relate the details of their adventurous trip to the hospital.

"And then he just kept going!" Nicola said.

"It wasn't really that big. Not even a crash. A literal fender-bender. But still . . ." Besnard said.

"He went right to the hospital! He didn't even stop!"

"Seven dollars and twenty-five cents on the meter. A record!"

As Grandmother Weird listened, her heart began beating faster. She held her grandson tighter. She wanted to cover his ears. She could not believe that his parents were mythologizing a moment of such irresponsibility and recklessness. She felt in her heart, her giant oversized heart, that this precious new Weird needed to be protected. She did not believe that his parents could do it. She knew that she wouldn't be around forever. Grandmother Weird concluded that this task would have to fall to him. Her desire for her grandchild to possess this power, the ability to keep safe, was so strong that it took shape within her. And then it tumbled out of her, and into him.

All of the Weird children had inklings that Richard possessed this ability. They suspected that in some significant way they fell under the umbrella of it as well. But they had no definitive proof until December 26, 1993, shortly before 4 p.m. The house on Palmerston Boulevard was filled with relatives, and after getting underfoot one time too many, the five of them were shoved into snowsuits and ski jackets, and into the backyard.

At the back of the yard there was an especially high snowbank, created by snow that had slid off the steep roof of the coach house. It was in this snowbank that the Weird siblings began to dig a tunnel. Abba and Kent worked from the south side. Lucy and Angie tunnelled from the north. Richard supervised from the outside, making sure that the two ends would meet up.

This was the winter that Besnard had started heating the coach house in an effort to preserve the Maserati. But the heat fled through the uninsulated roof as fast as the small heater pushed it out. The coach house remained cold. All Besnard had succeeded in creating was a row of long, pointy icicles, which hung directly over their tunnel. The afternoon had turned unseasonably warm, above zero, which made the snow wet and perfect for packing.

The tunnel was almost complete, with less than three feet separating the two teams of diggers. Richard suddenly felt an overwhelming compulsion to look up. He looked at the icicles. He looked down to where his siblings worked beneath the snow.

"Out now!" Richard screamed. "Everybody out now!"

There was something in his voice, a confidence, a complete lack of doubt that none of them could question. They scurried out of the tunnel. They ran as fast as they could across the backyard. They stopped just before the east wall of the house. They turned and looked back at the tunnel. Nothing happened.

"What?" Lucy demanded.

Then they heard a crack and all of the giant icicles fell from the roof. The tunnel was speared at sixteen different points.

"I hate it when you do that!" Lucy said.

"You hate it when I save your life?"

"You don't know that," Kent said. "They might have missed us."

"They would have speared your skulls!"

"Or maybe not. They could have missed."

"How could they? Look!" Richard said, pointing to the sixteen-time-speared tunnel.

"Still, you have no proof that you saved our lives," Lucy said.

"Not for sure," Kent said. Richard let out a very deep sigh.

And that's how it went. Even with proof as tangible as sixteen icicles, going along with Richard's predictions remained, for Lucy and Kent at least, an act of faith, every time. Although they always eventually went with what Richard said, they never stopped wondering what would have happened if they hadn't. Would the danger have been exactly as Richard predicted? How bad would the bad thing be? As the years progressed they began to wonder if being so careful all the time was actually the best course. It didn't seem to be working out all that well for Richard.

RICHARD, LUCY AND ANGIE STOOD so close to the automatic doors that their bodies triggered the sensors, keeping them open. Passengers gave jet-lagged sighs and wheeled their suitcases around them. Angie and Lucy didn't move until Richard put down his camera.

"You're not still letting Mother cut your hair?" he asked.

"You think I paid for this?" Lucy said.

"See, Lucy? Is this a coincidence?" Angie asked. Then she stepped forwards and hugged her older brother. Both her belly and the seven years of separation made this awkward.

"Wow!" he said.

"I'm pregnant. Not fat. Just so you know."

"You're beautiful," Richard said.

"The clock is ticking," Lucy said. She gestured towards the departures board to their right. Very near the top, their connecting flight aboard Airways Upliffta, flight AU812, was listed. There were forty-seven minutes before takeoff.

"This doesn't feel fated to you? This doesn't make you believe?" Angie asked her.

"It means nothing if you don't get him to come along," Lucy said.

"What are you two talking about?"

"Forty-six minutes . . ."

"Okay!" Angie said to Lucy. She took a very deep breath. "I went to see the Shark . . ." she said to Richard.

"Good God why?"

"That's exactly what I said."

"She's on her deathbed . . ."

"Again?"

"Listen to me!" Angie said. She stomped her foot. Her crazy hair flopped crazily around. "She told me that she blessed each of us at the moment of our births. But these blessings became curses and ruined our lives. In thirteen days . . ."

"Twelve."

"In twelve days, at the moment of her death, provided I gather the five of us in her hospital room, she will lift the curses, finally and forever."

"What did she say that she gave me?"

"That's it?" Lucy asked. "You're just buying that?"

"Self-protection," said Angie.

"Interesting," Richard said. He rubbed his thumb against his wedding ring, making it circle his finger.

"Lucy is directions. I'm forgiveness. Abba is hope. And Kent is, like, fighting. He's only strong when he's fighting."

"When exactly did you figure you'd swing by to pick me up?" Richard asked.

"Before Kent. Obviously before Kent," Angie said. "We'll need everybody if we're gonna get Kent."

"And how does she know she's going to die in twelve days?"

"It's her birthday."

"Perfect," Richard said. "What makes you believe her?"

"It just feels like truth. Doesn't it?" Angie asked.

"It certainly isn't fair," Richard said.

"We don't have much time," Lucy said. "You're either in or you're out."

"This does feel like a pretty big coincidence."

"I don't believe it for a second. I'm just going to see Abba. I'm only going as far as Abba," Lucy said.

"Isn't it time to see Abba? Isn't that much at least worth doing?"

"It is," Richard said. He picked up his suitcase. "I'll do it. I mean, I'll go like Lucy. I'll go as far as Abba."

"Oh Rich . . . ard!"

"Don't cry."

"I'm . . . not . . . crying."

"There's one condition."

"What?"

"Any . . . thing . . . Richard."

"You have to answer one question. Both of you. And you have to answer it truthfully."

"Y . . . es. Of course."

"How will you know if I don't answer it truthfully?"

"I'll know."

"What's the question?"

"Have you forgiven Dad?" Richard asked. Lucy looked at her feet. Angie looked at her stomach. They'd looked down for opposite reasons. And then Lucy looked up first.

"No," she said. "I haven't."

"Oh thank God," Richard said. "Thank God I'm not the only one."

Several quiet moments passed. And then, together, they walked to get Richard's ticket and the automatic doors finally closed.

W

HAVING LEFT RICHARD in first class, Angie and Lucy reached their seats in row 23. Angie realized that her sister had given her the window seat. She stopped. She did not stow her carry-on luggage in the overhead compartment. Passengers bunched up behind them.

"You do remember that I'm pregnant?"

"Who could forget that? You're huge."

"I want the aisle."

"Then you should have bought the tickets."

"That is so not fair."

"Truth isn't fair," she said, calmly.

Angie looked over Lucy's shoulder. The waiting passengers gave her no sympathy. Exaggerating the difficulty Angie pushed into the row and sat down in 23F. Lucy sat down beside her. They did not speak. Their silence continued as the flight attendant did her safety presentation. It remained as they fastened their seat belts for takeoff. Not a single word passed between them as the plane taxied down the runway. But just as the wheels left the ground, Lucy leaned over.

"You remember Zach Picard?" Lucy asked, loudly.

Angie raised her eyebrows. She slowly nodded her head. The back wheels left the ground.

"I fucked him."

"Recently?" Angie asked. The plane angled steeply as it climbed into the air.

"Not exactly."

"When exactly?"

"High school," Lucy said.

The wheels contracted into the plane. Angie's fingers curled into fists. "What grade?" she asked.

"Well, I was in Grade Eleven."

"But after he and I had broken up, though. Right?"

"Not exactly."

"While we were dating?"

"I'm afraid so," Lucy said.

The plane levelled out. The seat belt sign flashed off. Angie rushed down the aisle to the washroom and locked the door. She turned on the tap and pumped soap into her hands. A long repressed rage rose inside her, which she took out on her forearm.

The skin on Angie's arm turned red, yet the black marker remained. She shut off the tap. She stared at her reflection. She felt it slowly building inside her. It grew and grew and then it washed over her. The forgiveness flooded her from head to toe. She was filled with it. Absolutely and completely, without hesitation or resentment, Angie forgave Lucy. It was easy. It was beyond her control. It took more effort to dry her hands.

When she returned to row 23 Lucy had moved to the window seat, giving her the aisle. "Thanks," Angie said as she sat down.

"Are you being sarcastic?"

"No."

"Really, Angie? Really?"

"What?"

"You're not mad?"

"Oh. Zach?" Angie said. "That was shitty. You shouldn't have done that, Lucy. But, yes, I forgive you."

"Do you really mean it?"

"Of course," Angie said.

Lucy took her hands. She held them. She maintained eye contact for an uncomfortably long amount of time.

"Jesus Christ," Lucy said.

"What? What's wrong?"

"She did it. The Shark really did curse us," Lucy said. The plane hit a patch of turbulence. The seat belt sign flashed on. Lucy let go of Angie's hands and they both fastened themselves firmly into their seats.

THE ONLY BAGGAGE CAROUSEL in the Uplifftian
International Airport squeaked as it rotated. Angie and Lucy
and Richard watched it go around and around, even though
there wasn't a single suitcase on it. Local time was 2:15 p.m.
Angie was pretty sure it was April 9, although it was hard to
tell since Lucy had made them reset their watches during the
three-hour layover in Helsinki. She was definitely too tired
to figure it out. Dazed and jet-lagged, they waited for their
luggage, for anyone's luggage, to appear.

"I think I'm gonna be sick," Angie said and she had to
look away.

Their suitcases arrived thirty minutes later. They wheeled
them away from the baggage carousel and followed the other
passengers. As they walked past a row of uniformed men,
one of them reached for Lucy's purse, but Lucy clutched it
to her body and the men left her alone. Then they walked
through a set of automatic doors and found themselves
standing on the sidewalk in front of the airport.

"Where was customs?" Lucy asked.

"Maybe where that guy tried to see your purse?"

"But I pulled it away . . ." Lucy said. Angie shrugged her shoulders. Richard kicked a stone from the sidewalk. It rolled underneath the only taxi waiting.

According to their father's theory on the condition of taxis, accepting a ride in this cab would represent an exercise in self-loathing. Rust had eaten through its wheel wells. There was a sports sock where the right windshield-wiper blade should have been. Both doors were covered with an orange-coloured mud. They stood there for several minutes. But the taxi remained the only one available. Richard approached it. He opened the back passenger door on his fourth attempt. He got in and then Lucy held the door for Angie. She climbed in and sat beside Richard before she'd thought it through. "You know," Angie said, now sandwiched between her sister and her brother, "I'd like to remind both of you that I'm still pregnant."

"I'd like to remind you that there's no way for us not to see that."

"I was hoping that you'd bring that up, Angie. Have we met the father?"

"Are we ever going to?"

"I shouldn't have to be in the middle! Or have the window seat in planes! I shouldn't have to be doing any of this!"

"Ehrtr id iy yhsy you'f likr yo hoz?" the driver asked. They looked blankly at him and then blankly at each other.

"Right. The language."

"Did either of you think to bring a phrase book?"

"Is there such a thing?"

"English? Please?" Lucy said, loudly.

"Duvk my vuvk you dyupif Smericians. Rnhlidh noy yhr only boivrss," the driver said, loudly.

"We need to go to the Royal Palace."

"Queen Abba? Your queen? We're family."

"Take us to your leader!"

"Nice."

"Sentrill bizness diskrit!" the driver said.

"Close enough," Angie said.

The driver started the engine. The car jerked forward and they pulled away from the airport.

"I can't imagine taking a cab to Windsor Castle and asking to see Elizabeth," Lucy said.

"Do we even have her phone number? Can you just call the queen? Even here?" Angie asked.

"I seriously doubt that the royal standards in Upliffta and England are in any way comparable," Richard said. He loosened his tie and undid the top button on his dress shirt. A purple flowered crop none of them could name grew on both sides of the road. And there was an inescapable smell: pungent, fishy and unwelcoming. The closer they got to downtown the stronger it became.

"What is that stink?"

"Sewage?"

"Are they having a plague?"

The driver looked in the rear-view mirror. He made exaggerated sniffs with his nose. "Yhsy dmrll?" he asked.

"What is it?"

"Slönguskinn."

"What's *shlongskinn*?"

"Slönguskinn?" he repeated. He took his right hand off the wheel and moved it up and down in a wave-like motion.

"Terrible," Lucy said.

Even without the smell the back seat would have made Angie nauseous. Newspapers on the floor crunched under her feet. The windows were covered with grime. The stink of fish mixed with the smell of old cigarettes. The engine kept racing, making the car lurch forwards and then slow back down. Angie tried to focus on the hood ornament—which might have been an ox, it was hard to tell—but it didn't help.

"Stop the car!" Angie yelled.

"Ehsy?"

"Right now!"

"Pull over!"

"She needs to get out!"

"Trlsc! Trlsc!" our driver called. He pulled to the side of the road and stopped. Richard shuffled out. Angie followed, quickly. Three steps from the taxi she bent over and puked on the lovely purple flowers. She did it again. Then Angie glanced up and saw a large sign, which read:

WELCOME TO UPLIFFTA!
You won't regret your arrival!!

She looked back at the ground and puked again. It was the exclamation marks that did it. This was the first time in her life that Angie was prompted to regurgitate by punctuation. The driver turned on the radio. Richard and Lucy looked at each other and then they began to laugh.

"I'm sorry," Lucy said.

"I'm sorry too," Richard said. Neither stopped laughing.

"We always knew you were a crybaby . . ."

". . . and now you puke like a baby too!"

Angie looked up at them. She spit. She remained bent over, with her hands resting on her knees. She saw the billboard from the corner of her eye and she puked again.

The taxi didn't have power steering or power windows but the driver took Visa. Angie wasn't sure how much y576.78 was, but she was almost positive that she over-tipped. The driver helped them with their luggage and then they stood in downtown Upliffta. The tallest building was five storeys high. Most were two. There was only one stoplight in view. Their taxi drove underneath it, becoming the only vehicle on the road.

"Maybe they really are having a plague," Richard said.

"What do we do now?"

"It's over here," Lucy said. She pointed to her right. Without looking back Lucy marched across the street. Richard and Angie shrugged. They looked left and then right. No cars were visible in either direction and they hurried across the road.

Every store was closed. The streets were narrow and mainly in shadow. The cars parked on them were rusty and unfamiliar. They saw no people as they walked. And then from quite far away they heard a large crowd cheering. Richard and Angie stopped. Lucy continued for half a block before she noticed that her siblings lingered behind.

"Come on!" she yelled.

"Maybe we should go that way?" Angie asked. "Towards the possibility of humanity?"

"But the palace is this way. We're really close."

"Are you sure?"

"Isn't that why we're here?"

"I'm just here to see Abba," Richard said. He took his phone out of his pocket. He had no service. "But where is here?"

"It's less than six blocks away. I promise you," Lucy said. She walked away briskly. Several moments later Angie and Richard began to follow her again.

They walked past a house that leaned to the left. A large chunk of the road ahead of them was missing.

"I think these cars are Soviet," Richard said.

"Where the hell are we?" Angie asked.

"I'm suddenly much less envious that my sister is the queen of this," Lucy said.

"Queen of Shithole-ia!" Richard said.

Angie laughed. Then she ran into Lucy's back. Lucy did not move. Angie stepped around her. She saw what had caused her sister to freeze.

"I just got envious again," Lucy said.

"Is that what I think it is?" Angie asked.

"Full scale," Richard answered.

"How the hell did she do that?"

"She is the queen . . ."

"She *is* the queen . . ."

They nodded their heads, unaware that they did this in unison. None of them could really believe it, yet there it was, right in front of them, towering seven storeys high: an exact, fully realized, life-sized version of Abba's castle.

THE RAINYTOWN TOWN COUNCIL Planning Development and Construction Committee met every fourth day it rained. Proposals for new buildings were required to include sketches, approximate dimensions and notes on how the structure would improve life for the citizens of Rainytown on both an economic and social level. All five of the Weird children had a vote and for the first two summers everyone's proposals were automatically passed and built. Then they ran out of floor space and everything changed, since every proposal for a new building meant that a pre-existing one had to be torn down.

Debates began to rage. They all wanted to see their own buildings preserved. At the same time they wanted their new proposals to be green-lit. Alliances were made and deals were struck.

Only Abba, noble of heart, hoping that their better natures would emerge, refused to participate in what she called the corruption of Rainytown. Which meant she had no allies. So they were all shocked when, with only two weeks left of summer vacation and Kent calling for new proposals, Abba moved to the front of the room. Lucy had already agreed to support Angie's proposal for the Purple Magic Roller Disco Palace, while Richard was putting his vote behind Kent's Jungle Cat Galaxy, a combination zoo and planetarium. None of them had time for whatever it was that Abba was about to go on about. Her right hand was holding several pieces of lined white paper and it visibly trembled. Kent raised his wrist and pointed to a watch that wasn't there.

"Well?" Richard asked.

"I think what Rainytown needs more than anything else . . ." Abba said. She looked down. She looked back up. "Is a castle!"

The rain could be heard hitting the roof. No one moved. Neither Richard nor Abba nor Lucy nor even Angie had ever thought this big before. Some kind of barrier, invisible and self-imposed, had been shattered. Abba passed around her sketches and no one said a single word and then they all spoke at once.

"Fantastic!"

"It'll be, like, twice as high as anything we've made."

"Three times."

"We could use real frosting for the pink walls."

"It's like another level. It's Rainytown squared!"

"That doesn't make sense."

"Could it have a disco roller rink?" Angie asked.

"The Purple Magic Roller Disco Palace!" Abba agreed.

"Can we put it here? Around back?"

"Sure!"

"It's a massive undertaking."

"Can we put it to a vote?"

"I don't think we need to," Kent said. Even though it necessitated the demolition of the Tragedy Strikes Bowling Alley, It's Curtains for You Interior Design and the C.U. Soohn Funeral Home, construction commenced immediately.

THE QUEEN OF UPLIFFTA SWEPT her waist-length red hair out of her face and tried to make eye contact with her subjects as they parted to let her through. These attempts were unsuccessful. The citizens stared at the ground. On each side of her were four guards in red uniforms. The golden tassels attached to their shoulders fluttered as they walked. When they reached the front of the crowd the guards lifted her up onto a wooden stage.

Queen Abba raised her arms. The crowd, which had been silent, began to cheer. A red velvet curtain was raised, revealing a large glass aquarium. The tank was the size of a car. Inside it a mass of slönguskinn twisted their dark, limbless bodies and snapped their sharp pointed teeth.

Abba climbed six steps and stood on a raised platform behind the aquarium. She looked down into the open water. Slönguskinn broke the surface and then dove back down again. Abba rolled up the sleeve of her purple robe. She raised her right hand. She plunged her arm into the putrid brown water.

The queen smiled; little in the world disgusted her more than slönguskinn. She loathed their slippery bodies. She feared their tooth-filled mouths. A species of saltwater eel, they were the pillar of Upliffta's economy, but their stink turned Abba's stomach and their shiny black eyes haunted her sleep. The queen's smile grew in proportion to her revulsion as she thrust her arm deeper into the tank.

The first one she grasped squirmed away. The second bit her and she let it go. She plunged her other hand into the tank and, using both hands, Abba clutched one and held it firmly. Brackish water splashed onto her face as she pulled it out of the water. The eel twisted and bucked. Its mouth snapped open and closed. Its unblinking black eyes stared down. Abba tightened her grip and raised the fish over her head. The crowd cheered. She slammed the wiggling length of it onto a butcher's block.

Putting her hand behind its neck, Abba pinned the creature down. The slönguskinn twisted its head as it tried to bite her. Abba tightened her grip. She held out her right hand. A guard rushed to place the handle of a wooden mallet in her palm. Abba raised her arm. She brought the mallet down. She hit the slönguskinn's head and the creature stopped moving.

This is where the ceremony normally would have ended. Yet Abba raised her arm once more. She brought the mallet down with even greater force. She swung it a third time. She swung it a fourth. She swung again and again and again.

She continued striking the slönguskinn until there was very little of it left to hit.

Raising her head the queen looked over the crowd. It was smaller than last year's. It was the smallest in memory. She thrust her arms over her head anyway. "Rrl hunyinh drsdon id slönguskinn noe oggivislly oprn!" she yelled. By uttering this phrase she had officially declared the slönguskinn fishing season open.

"May it be my last," Abba whispered.

The mallet fell from her hand and the guards carried her down into the crowd, which had already begun to part for her.

THE FENCE THAT SURROUNDED Abba's castle was wrought iron and elaborate but not very tall, not even seven feet high. Angie, Richard and Lucy stood in front of it. They looked through the black bars at the pink castle. "It must be electrified," Lucy said.

"You think?" Richard asked. He reached out his hands and grabbed it. His body shook. His eyes rolled back in his head. Spittle flew from his lips.

"Oh my God!" Lucy yelled.

"Stop it! Stop it!" Angie yelled.

"Sorry," Richard said. He stopped the shaking and the eye-rolling. He took his hands off the bars. "Couldn't resist."

"Very nice."

"Not cool."

"I said I'm sorry. But look," Richard said. He grabbed the bars and let go. He did this several times. "It's just a fence. There's no charge."

Richard looked at Lucy. They both put their hands on the bars and began to climb. "Um, hello?" Angie called. Neither of her siblings stopped. Richard swung his legs over the top. Lucy did the same. They both jumped, landing directly in front of Angie on the other side of the fence.

"Just wait here," Richard said.

"Wow. When's the last time I heard that? Grade Seven? Grade Eight?"

"We'll be right back. I promise."

"Nice. Really nice, guys."

"Don't stray," Lucy said.

"I'm not twelve."

"Then stop acting like you are," Lucy said. She put her hand through the bars; Angie didn't take it, and Lucy took it away.

"I hope there's dogs," Angie yelled. Lucy and Richard ran towards the castle. They did not look back. As they disappeared behind a stand of trees Angie forgave them. She sat down on their luggage. She stared up at Abba's castle. The longer Angie looked the more she felt like she'd shrunk. As if she were actually inside Rainytown. She had an urge to pick at the grass and see if there was cardboard underneath. The castle was perfect in every detail. So perfect that Angie began to wonder about the Purple Magic Roller Disco Palace.

Against Lucy's advice Angie began to stray. She followed the black fence. At the rear of the castle she found a gate. Angie pushed it. The gate swung open. "Doesn't anybody lock anything around here?" she said out loud and then she stepped inside the grounds. No one tried to stop her. She followed a path of purple stones. At the top of a small hill she could see it. For several moments Angie stood and stared at it. The building was instantly recognizable for three reasons; it was oval, it was purple, and there was a giant pair of roller skates on the roof.

"No way," Angie said and then she ran towards it.

The front door was made of glass. Angie cupped her hands over her eyes and looked inside. The walls were covered with fake purple fur. Behind a long counter rose row after row of roller skates. On the floor, tiled in handwriting that looked suspiciously like hers were the words:

PURPLE MAGIC ROLLER DISCO PALACE

Angie tried the door. She found it unlocked. She opened it and went inside. It took a while to discover the switch underneath the left end of the counter. When she flicked it everything turned on all at once. Red and green lights shone from the ceiling. Disco music played through hidden speakers, filling the air with the sounds of KC and the Sunshine Band. A mirror ball turned in the middle of the rink and tiny squares of light drifted across the walls and the floor.

Angie searched the shelves until she found a pair of size six roller skates. She laced them on, tightly. She took slow careful steps to the edge of the rink. "Listen," she said, looking down at her belly, "if you're gonna stay with me, these are the types of risks we're gonna have to take."

She stepped onto the rink. Taking tiny strides Angie moved slowly. She held her stomach with both of her hands. She sang along with the music. She made three full revolutions. The song ended and another one followed. She couldn't remember the name of the singer, it was something Spanish, but she knew the song was called *Born to Be Alive*.

Angie sang along to this song too. It wasn't hard. The lyrics consisted mainly of repeating the phrase, "born to be alive." Her arms fell to her sides. Her strides became longer. By the second chorus she was snapping her fingers to the beat and wiggling her hips.

Her confidence returned. She started doing cross-steps around the corners. At the far end of the rink she took six long strides and gathered speed. She closed her eyes, held out her arms and glided. The wind blew back her hair. She sailed the length of the rink. When she opened her eyes she saw Abba standing against the boards.

Using the toe brake Angie stopped, quickly. She turned and skated back to where Abba stood. The toes of Angie's roller skates touched the bottom of the boards. Her stomach touched her sister's.

"Are you real?" Abba asked. She reached out her hand and touched Angie's face and then they both began to cry.

W

MANY THINGS SURPRISED RICHARD and Lucy as the red-uniformed guards marched them into the dining room. They didn't expect the cathedral ceiling, the suits of armour or the family crests. Angie wanted to believe that the biggest shock to her siblings would be seeing her beside the massive stone fireplace. It wasn't. What threw them was Abba. She stood perfectly still and said nothing, yet some sort of grace radiated from her. Their tomboyish sister had been transformed into a queen.

The guards stopped, forcing Richard and Lucy to stop too. The log in the fireplace popped. The room was otherwise silent. Having failed to convince the royal guards that they were siblings of the queen, Lucy and Richard had spent several hours locked in a small windowless room. Lucy was upset, but not about that.

"Eight years?" Lucy yelled.

"That's your greeting?' Abba replied.

"You don't call once in eight years?"

"Hello? You're not surprised that I'm here? That I strayed

and by straying I found her before you did?" Angie asked. All three of them ignored her.

"If I remember correctly," Abba said, calmly, "the phones in Canada dial out."

"You missed birthdays and Christmases and Mom going nuts!"

"Well, happy belated birthdays. You always said you hated Christmas. Mom was always nuts."

"You didn't even invite us to your wedding! Were you embarrassed of us or were you just ashamed of your . . . your . . . *provincial* origins?"

"I was under the impression that you were all dead," Abba said. She said this in a cold matter-of-fact way, which made even Lucy pause. The fire popped again. "Apparently I was misinformed."

"Why did you think we were dead?" Lucy asked.

"Let's just leave that for now," Abba said.

"It's great to see you," Richard said, "but I agree that you have some explaining to do."

"Explain yourself!"

"Don't act so righteous with me, Lucy Weird," Abba said. Her voice became solid and firm and sad. "When Dad died you disappeared into yourself and left me on my own. You were my big sister. You should have been there for me. You too, Richard. But neither of you were, so I took care of myself. Don't blame me if I left you behind. I did what I had to do."

Abba continued to stare straight ahead. Lucy and Richard looked at the floor.

"That doesn't make it right," Lucy said. Her eyes watched her hands.

"No, it doesn't," Abba said. "But once I got used to doing it that way there was no going back."

"It was a stressful time," Lucy said.

"For all of us," Angie said.

"As it always is for the Weirds," Richard said. The guards released him. Pulling out a chair, he sat at the long wooden table. He plucked a red linen napkin off a bone white plate. He spread it over his lap. He did these things with such calmness and confidence that the rest of his siblings had no choice but to follow his lead. This made Angie love him just a little bit more.

"Can we get these candles lit?" Richard asked.

Abba looked at a guard. He lit the candles. Waiting until her siblings were in their chairs, Abba sat at the head of the table. Her posture was breathtaking. "How is Kent?" she asked.

"We don't know."

"We think he's still living on Palmerston."

"Mother?"

"Living in a nursing home, convinced she's a hairdresser, but otherwise the same."

"Lucy and I just saw her in Winnipeg. She cut our hair! Claimed not to recognize either of us."

"That explains how you look."

"When do we get to meet the king?" Richard asked.

"I'm afraid that he's dead," she said. Her shoulders slouched.

"Oh."

"I'm sorry."

"We didn't know."

"How about *your* husband?" Abba asked Angie. The guards began filling their glasses with red wine.

"She doesn't have one," Richard said.

"Our sister seems to have become a woman of easy virtue," Lucy said.

"Look who's talking," Abba said.

"Thank you," Angie said. "Do you have any children?"

"Not yet," Abba said. She exhaled. Her posture straightened. "Should I wait until after dinner to ask why you've come?"

"That," Richard said, "is an idea as good as this wine."

The meal was roast beef, overdone, with scalloped potatoes. Angie didn't have any coffee, of course, but no one who did asked for a second cup. The plainness of the meal was more than dwarfed by Angie's joy at being in a country where they didn't refuse to fill a pregnant woman's wineglass. She let it be refilled three times. This was a fraction of what her siblings drank.

"Velll?" Abba asked. It was long after the plates had been cleared.

"Is that an accent or are you shlurring?"

"What is *shlurring*?"

"What's the story? What's brought you here?"

"Let me this time!" Lucy shouted.

"Angie went to see the Shark!" Richard shouted, louder.

"Good God why?"

"That's exactly what I said!"

"The Shark claims," Lucy said, "that at the moment of our births she blessed each of us with a supernatural power that has since cursed us and ruined our lives. I call them blursings."

"Blessing plus curse equals blursing?"

"Yes."

"Very nice."

"Thank you. The Shark also claims that she will die on her birthday and that all five of us must be in her hospital room so she can lift the blursings at the moment she expires."

"Well done," Richard said. He raised his glass. "That was much more succinct than Angie's version."

"How very *Sharky*," Abba said.

"Don't you wanna know the powers?" Angie asked.

"Can I guess?"

"Please."

"Lucy. Well it's obviously the directions thing. Angie, also easy, you forgive everyone."

"Two for two."

"Richard . . . you can predict the future? Sense impending doom?"

"Self-preservation."

"That's it."

"It's a sword, double-edged."

"Don't you wanna know what she gave to you?"

"Oh, I already know."

"Do you?"

Abba's glass was half empty. She drank what remained. She stood up. "It's hope," she said. "I never seem able to give up hope." She threw her glass into the fireplace. It shattered. She fell back into her chair. Her shoulders slumped and she stared at the middle of the table, seeming to forget that any of them were there.

W

Shortly after midnight Angie, Richard and Lucy were each assigned a member of the Royal Guard, who escorted them to their rooms. The guard who went with Lucy was by far the best looking. On the fifth floor he opened the door to her room. Lucy leaned forwards. She looked inside. There was a large four-poster bed, opulent purple drapes and a crystal chandelier. Extending her right foot Lucy tapped her toe on the marble floor inside her room. Then she took two steps closer to the guard.

"Know any good bars?" Lucy asked.

"Yes," the guard said. His English had no trace of an accent. "I know several."

Forty-three minutes later Lucy realized that she knew neither the name of the bar—the washroom of which she was in—nor the name of the man underneath her. She ran her fingers through the golden tassels attached to his shoulders.

"Fifteen," he said. "Fourteen."

"What's it like . . ." Lucy asked. She bit his ear with tender and then considerable force.

"Twelve . . . eleven."

". . . to *fuck* the queen's sister?"

"Sure. Yes. Okay."

"You don't believe me?"

"Nine. I do. Of course. It's just that . . . eight."

"What?"

"Nothing. Seven."

"What?" Lucy repeated. She stopped. The stiffness in her limbs indicated that she wouldn't continue until he did.

"Well. Yes. Husband was a very rich . . . yes . . . a very rich man."

"Yes . . . and?"

"Very powerful."

"Keep counting."

"Six. Five. Owned everything. Four. The country. Rich enough to be king. Three. But. No king."

"What about the castle? The guards? The uniforms?"

"Two. Upliffta has no king."

"It's all pretend?"

"Yes!" the man screamed, although Lucy did not know if this was in response to her question or her body.

Richard lay in bed on top of the covers. He turned on the television. He surfed through the channels. There were seven.

Each aired an American drama. He recognized these shows from his youth. The dubbing was horrible. The novelty of watching familiar TV in a foreign language wore off, quickly. He began to change the channel each time a scene ended. He pretended that everything he saw was part of the same TV show. He couldn't make much sense of it, but then again he could say the same thing about his life.

"I need you to help me dig up my husband," Abba said.

There was a lamp on Angie's bedside table. She turned it on. The light woke her up a bit more. She had been in a deep sleep, her first in twenty-four hours. Maybe more. The time shifts made it hard to tell. Squinting, she saw that her sister was perched on the side of her bed. Angie rubbed her eyes. When she took her hands away from her face, Abba was still there.

"How did you even get in here?" Angie asked.

"Nobody locks anything around here. It's weird. But Angie, I'm pleading with you. Will you do it?"

"Ask me again?"

"Will you help me dig up my husband?"

"I thought I hadn't heard you right."

"I really need your help."

"Are you drunk?"

"I'm desperate," Abba said. She looked down at her hands. "My husband told me that you were dead. That all of you were dead."

"You weren't lying about that?"

"He showed me newspaper articles."

"What did we die of?"

"Why would you ask that?"

"Why wouldn't I?"

"The furnace in the house on Palmerston leaked carbon monoxide and killed you all while you slept."

"Not a bad way to go. What about the Shark?"

"She suffered a massive stroke at your funeral and died days later."

"All this was in the paper?"

"He showed me an entire issue of the *Globe and Mail*. It made the front page."

"I guess that could be faked . . ."

"I even got a call from Mr. Winters. He expressed his condolences."

"Who?"

"The dispatcher. From Grace Taxi."

"Why him?"

"I guess he could be bought. You can see why I'm a little *fucked up* right now."

"I don't think I've ever heard you swear."

"Angie! Are you getting this?"

"I am. I'm just trying to take it in slowly."

"That's why you didn't get invited to the wedding. Why I never called or wrote or visited."

"You didn't Google us or anything? I mean, Richard is pretty well known. He's some kind of famous photographer, although they all look like snapshots to me."

"That's the thing," Abba said. She took both of Angie's hands. "I did. Constantly. Daily."

"He blocked Weird? Can you do that? I mean, is that even possible?"

"I no longer know what he is capable of."

"So you think . . ."

"Yes, I do. If I don't see it with my own eyes I'll never be sure. I'll always hope. I'll be stuck in hope forever."

"Do you still hope that Dad's alive?" Angie asked.

"I don't know for sure that he isn't," Abba said. "Neither do you!"

"Abba, even the insurance company agreed that the fall from the cliff would have been fatal."

"But they never found him. No body, no proof!" Abba said. Angie said nothing.

During weaker moments all the Weird children had taken comfort in the idea that their father had somehow survived. But in Abba it had been different. Hope for the others had been a place of last resort. Abba's hope was something she lived inside of. Subtly, they had encouraged her. It had seemed very important that someone kept this hope alive. It made sense to Angie, in a Weird way, that Abba would now be doing it for her dead husband.

"It's just . . . this is asking a lot, Abba."

"I know it is. That's why I'm asking you."

"If I agree to do it . . . at least to get Richard to do it . . . you know I'm going to ask you to come with us to see the Shark."

"I figured that would be the trade-off."

"You're the only one who isn't afraid of Kent."

"He isn't as scary as you guys make him out."

"Ah, Abba. Still. I'm not sure if I can."

"Knowing what you know, about me, about us, can you really say no?" Abba asked.

Angie looked down at her sister's slender pink toes. She sat up in the bed. She decided not to do it. Then the baby kicked and she knew that she had to.

ON THE MORNING OF MAY 17, 2002, five months and three weeks after the disappearance of their father had been reported, the five Weird siblings sat around their infrequently used dining room table, staring at their plates. Angie poked her eggs with a knife. The yolks broke and oozed onto her undercooked bacon. She pushed her plate away.

"If she's gonna pretend this is a hotel," Richard said as he took his napkin from his lap, folded it carefully and set it on the table, "she could at least hire a cook."

"*Fuck* you," Kent said. He had done the cooking. He stood and went to the window.

"What's that?" Lucy asked.

"Where's it coming from?" Abba asked.

"Come take a *fucking* look at this," Kent said, as a mechanical beeping filled the room.

They rushed to the window and they did not like what they saw: a police tow truck was backing their father's Maserati into their driveway.

For five months and two weeks the car had been kept as evidence. This was the first time any of them had seen it. The back end looked untouched. The front was severely crumpled. Just above the steering wheel there was a basketball-sized hole in the windshield. Angie tried to figure out how it got there. Then she remembered that her father never wore his seat belt and she tried not to look at it. The tow truck stopped. The driver got out. He pulled a lever. They held their breaths as the front tires lowered. When the wheels touched the asphalt, they all breathed out. The tow truck's passenger door opened and Detective Jennifer McKay climbed out.

No one was ever able to figure out why Detective McKay had taken such a personal interest in the death of Besnard Weird. Somewhat exceeding her authority, she'd used the fact that Besnard's body had never been recovered to keep the case open even after the insurance company was convinced it had been an accident. The Weird siblings watched her from the bay window as she walked up to the front door of their house. Detective McKay rang the bell. None of them moved. She rang it again. She saw them watching from the bay window and she kept the button depressed. They waited just a little bit longer and then, slowly, they walked to the front door.

Using her fingers Lucy began counting to ten. The buzzer continued to ring. When Lucy's last finger was extended, Richard opened the door, quickly.

"Detective Decay," he sang, "how wonderful to see you!"

"We're releasing the Maserati," Detective McKay said.

"Funny how that's happening today," Richard said.

"These things happen," Detective McKay continued. "We're so sorry to interrupt your special day."

What made this day special was their father's funeral. The five-month-and-three-week delay had been caused by numerous factors: the nervous breakdown of their mother, the disorder of their finances, a continuing police investigation and Abba's urgings to wait just a little longer, in the hope that their father's body would be found. But Richard demanded that the service happen before May 23. He could live with having waited *almost* half a year. But he couldn't stand the idea of having waited *over* half a year. And even Abba agreed.

"Will you be able to attend?" Richard asked, loudly.

"Sorry, I've got prior commitments," Detective McKay said. She extended a clipboard and a pen. "We're releasing the car. Perhaps your mother could sign for it?"

"As you well know, our mother is incapacitated by the demands of modern living," Richard said. He signed his name. He handed Detective McKay the clipboard and put the pen in his pocket.

"My condolences," she said as she tucked the clipboard under her arm. She turned to leave. Then she stopped. From the inside pocket of her jacket, she pulled a thick envelope. It was clearly marked as being from the City of Toronto and the very size of it projected a sense of legality and doom.

Detective McKay held it out to Richard. She was smiling. "How could I have almost forgotten this?"

"Moonlighting as a mailwoman?" Richard asked as he snapped the envelope from her hand.

"Sorry. While I was waiting I thought I might as well pick up your mail for you. I suspect it isn't a refund," Detective McKay said. She closed the door herself and Richard opened the envelope, which contained a thick set of pink papers.

"What is it?"

"Hold on . . ."

"What does it say?"

"According to this . . ." Richard said. In the silence that followed they heard the tow truck pull out of the driveway. "We have ninety days to come up with a hundred and twenty thousand dollars of back taxes or the house becomes the property of the city of Toronto."

This was not the first time that the Weird children had cause to suspect the state of their father's finances. For one thing, Besnard paid for everything in cash—movies, restaurants, gas, it all came from a thick roll of bills he always carried in his front right pocket. If Nicola needed money for groceries, or they needed money for anything, he simply took out this billfold and started peeling off currency.

It was possible that the Grace Taxi Service was a much more lucrative concern than they imagined. The Weirds did live awfully well for a family whose sole income came from a small business with a large overhead. They certainly lived much better than their grandparents, who had been supported by the very same enterprise.

And then—close to the end of Besnard's life—men who did not seem to be his normal business associates began appearing at their door, late at night. After ten and sometimes later, a rough knock would echo through the house on Palmerston Boulevard. Besnard would rush to answer it. The children only caught glimpses of these men, if they saw them at all. They were never invited inside the house. Besnard would step outside and then lead them to the coach house. There they would talk, sometimes for a few minutes and sometimes for an hour.

No matter how long he was gone, when Besnard came back inside he always did the same thing. He'd walk into the living room and commandeer the television. Even if his children were in the middle of a program they'd deemed profoundly important, he would turn on the VCR, a technology that, even in 2001, seemed outdated. Besnard would put in a tape and watch pre-recorded episodes of *Sunny Day Motel*. This was a half-hour situation comedy originally broadcast in the early seventies, starring Danny Day as a hapless motel owner. Each tape held three episodes. He'd be on his third or fourth when the rest of his family went up to bed.

These were the only times their father ever watched TV.

———

Six hours after the visit from Detective McKay the Weird children stood behind a hearse at the back of St. James Cemetery. The hearse was parked at the top of a small hill. At the bottom of the slope was the black rectangular shape of their father's open grave. The sun was bright and the sky was blue, and Richard and Kent had begun to bicker.

"Kent, listen to me," Richard said. "You cannot be at the back. It's not safe. I need to be at the back."

"Not this time, Ricky. You are not pulling that *shit* on me this time."

"Damn it, Kent! Listen to me!"

"It's not like it's super heavy! The girls could carry it on their own!"

"Kent! This is important," Richard said, loudly. The twelve people sitting amongst the forty chairs at the bottom of the hill tried not to look. Except for Grandmother Weird, whose menacing glare was a physical manifestation of *the Tone*.

"This is really important," Richard whispered.

"I don't care!"

"Enough," Angie said. She stepped between them. "Here's the deal. Kent, you're the youngest. You had the shortest amount of time with him, so you get to go at the back and be the last to hold him."

"Vote," Lucy said.

"This is bigger than a vote!" Richard said.

"Who's for Angie's deal?"

Richard was the only one not to raise a hand. "You don't understand . . ."

"Richard—the vote has been taken," Lucy said.

"You guys are gonna be sorry."

"Exactly why are we going to be sorry?" Kent asked.

Richard didn't have an answer. He took the front handle and pulled the casket towards him. Abba went to the right side. Lucy and Angie took the left. They walked forwards and then the coffin came off the track and out of the hearse and Kent took hold of the back.

What happened next was the intersection of two unrelated factors. The first was that the caretaker had just watered the lawn, which none of the Weirds had noticed. The second was that Kent's shoes, which had been their father's, were extremely worn at the soles. Six steps down the slope, Kent's slippery shoes met the wet grass and, without warning, he went down. The back of the coffin fell with him. Lucy and Angie were suddenly carrying more weight than they expected. Knocked off balance, they fell too. Abba went next. This left Richard, trying to hold the casket all by himself.

At first it looked like he might do it. He turned quickly. He put his right shoulder under the corner. He steadied the side with his left hand and slid his right arm as far underneath it as he could. His forearms flexed. His fingers curled. For a split second the casket seemed to hover in the air, defying gravity. Then the far end began to descend, pulling it out of Richard's hands.

It twisted as it fell, and struck the ground at a 45-degree angle. The lid sprang open, revealing to everyone present an aqua-blue satin interior and nothing else.

If just one of the Weirds had been able to see the absurdity in this tragedy, the rest of them would have as well. But none of the Weird siblings were, in this moment, strong enough to be as outrageous as the circumstances they found themselves in. They just stood there. And then they scattered.

Richard ran as fast as he could. He ran towards the cemetery gates. He kept running after he ran through them.

Abba kicked off her shoes. Barefoot, carrying her footwear by the straps, her naked pink toes curling in the grass, she walked back up the hill towards the hearse.

Kent beat her to it. He sat in the passenger seat of the hearse.

Lucy followed Richard towards the cemetery gates, but she did not run. She walked at a leisurely pace. Those close to her heard her humming. No one realized that the song was "Temptation" by New Order.

Only Angie stayed where she was, forgiving them, instantly. Stepping forwards she closed the lid. Her knees were still bent. She looked at the tiny, mortified crowd. Only her grandmother was looking away. Angie caught the eyes of John Winters, the dispatcher of the Grace Taxi

Company. Mr. Winters gathered four of the men sitting around him. They stood and surrounded the casket. They lifted it easily. They carried her father's empty coffin to her father's empty grave.

THE GATE TO THE UPLIFFTIAN Royal Cemetery was unlocked. The graveyard was surrounded on three sides by a black iron fence and on the fourth by the ocean. The fence was not rusty. Despite the damp sea air, no moss grew on any of the headstones. Several of the graves were dated from the 1800s, yet they looked no worse for wear than the stones from the 1900s. Abba was the only one who didn't notice these things.

Holding a lantern, Abba led the way. Behind her, Richard carried a shovel. Next came Lucy. In her left hand was a crowbar. Angie came last. She carried only her daughter. At the foot of the grave closest to the water Abba set down the lantern. Her husband's monument was an enormous black stone. The epitaph read:

LUTIVEN VIJA

MAY 24TH, 1945–DECEMBER 8TH, 2007

The only thing he loves more than Upliffta is her Queen.

Angie couldn't help notice that the epitaph was in the present tense. She did not mention this. She looked at Richard. He held out the shovel.

"Don't be an ass," Lucy said.

"Okay, you're right," Richard said. He nodded, turned and raised the shovel to Abba.

"Don't be a bigger ass!" Lucy said.

"Then you do it!"

"Richard!"

"But . . ." Richard said. Then he fell silent. The propane lantern hissed. He turned his back to his sisters. He looked at the ocean. His shoulders were hunched up. They stayed this way for several moments. Then they relaxed and he turned around and pushed the shovel through the grass and he began to dig.

Angie stood for as long as she could. Then she sat on the grass, which was wet. She watched Richard dig. The bigger the pile of dirt got, the less of him she could see. Only the top of his head remained visible when the shovel hit something solid. Richard reached up, Lucy passed him the crowbar and Angie looked at her hands. She counted the blades of grass that were stuck to her fingers as she heard the wood splinter. Then no one said anything, which made her look back up.

Abba was on her knees at the foot of the grave. "Thank God," Abba said, quietly, and then she began to sob.

Nobody helped Richard climb out of the grave. There was dirt on his face and under his fingernails. The crowbar was still in his hand as he walked towards Angie. He tossed the crowbar. It landed at her feet.

"At least we know where one father figure is," Richard said.

He walked to the cemetery gates and through them. Lucy began shovelling dirt back into the hole. Abba silently wept. Angie put her hands on her stomach and she did not look away. She didn't join them either.

A LARGE PORTION OF THE departures area of the Upliffta International Airport was roped off because a truck-sized chunk of concrete had fallen from the ceiling. Inside the perimeter two men worked a jackhammer. They were attempting to break the large chunk into smaller pieces and succeeding in creating a lot of dust and noise.

Covering their mouths, Angie, Lucy, Richard and Abba walked around the mess. They were almost at the other side when Angie saw the man who was waiting for them. Or at least for her. He held a bouquet of the purple roadside flowers. His suit was well tailored but rumpled. As Angie's siblings rushed ahead, he ran up to her.

"Angie!" he called, loudly. The jackhammering continued as he got down on one knee and extended the flowers. "I've been so worried about you."

Angie neither looked down nor stopped. She walked around him and joined her siblings at a special ticket counter that had been opened for the queen and her family. She continued ignoring him, even when he appeared at her side.

"HEY! JUST TALK TO ME!" he screamed. The jack-hammer fell silent and his raised voice echoed off the concrete roof. At the front of the line Richard turned around. He looked at the guy and then he looked at Angie. Dropping his suitcase Richard stepped between his sister and the man she was pretending not to know.

"This guy bugging you?" Richard asked.

"I don't even know who you're talking about," Angie said. She wished that the men operating the jackhammer would get back to work.

"This guy. This guy right here."

"I don't see anyone."

"Right here! The one with the flowers."

"Ah, Richard, sometimes you can be so thick!"

"Excuse me?"

"Who is this guy?" Lucy asked, having wandered back from her place in line.

"Who are you?" Abba demanded, having followed Lucy.

"I'm her husband!"

"You are not my husband!"

"Well, you can't deny I'm the father of your unborn child!" he said. He looked at her siblings who had all gathered around. "Who the hell are you people?"

Angie's undeniable compulsion to instantly forgive every-body made love very difficult for her. Her heart had been broken over and over again. The men she fell in love with tended to take advantage of her forgiving nature. Eventually they lost respect for her, thinking that she had no respect for herself.

Angie had become afraid of love. Her solution was Paul. He was, in fact, her husband as well as the father of her unborn child. She definitely was in love with him. But he was also someone she could keep at an emotional arm's length. Or to put it another way, treat like shit and be assured that he would never leave her.

At the time, Angie thought Paul let her treat him like this because he had low self-esteem. She had no idea it was because he loved her more than anyone ever had, or ever would.

Angie walked past her husband, stepped up to the counter and checked her luggage. The rest of the Weirds did the same. Leaving Paul behind, they proceeded to security. Angie presented her boarding pass to the uniformed official. She did not look over her shoulder as she put her keys and change into a plastic tray. She took off her running shoes. The metal detector didn't beep as she passed through it, but the baby gave her stomach a good kick. Then another one, which turned into a series of kicks, each one slightly harder than the last.

"Okay," Angie said, looking down at her stomach. "Okay, okay, okay," she repeated. She looked through the metal detector. Richard and Lucy hadn't walked through it yet.

"Really?" Angie called towards them. She held her shoes with her hands. The laces flapped around as she spoke. "Not one of you is going to do this for me?"

"Do what?" Richard called.

"Really?" Angie continued. "Really?"

"What?" Lucy said.

"I'm really going to have to say it? I'm going to have to ask?"

"What are you talking about, Angie?"

"Jesus!"

"What? What aren't we doing?"

"Just go get him! Will you not just go get him?"

"The guy with the flowers?"

"Who wasn't your husband?"

"Yes. That guy. Please go and get him."

"Who is he?"

"He's my husband," Angie said. "He's the love of my life."

Neither Lucy nor Richard said another word. They nodded their heads. They put their shoes back on. Stepping out of line, they walked back towards the front of the airport. "His name is Paul. You'll probably have to buy him a ticket," Angie called after them.

Kent Weird pushed a shopping cart dangerously overloaded with empty beer and wine bottles up the middle of Palmerston Boulevard. His clothes were dirty. His beard was long and unkempt. The cart bounced over every crack in the road. The bottles rattled. He steadied the empties with his left hand and he steered with his right hand. Yet the majority of his attention was given over to finding an imaginative way to kill himself.

He knew the method had to be unique and original and unlike anything that anyone had ever done before. It had to be everything that Kent felt he wasn't and wished he were. His current favourite plan involved placing eight running chainsaws at the bottom of a tall building. Then Kent would swan dive from the top and land on the chainsaws. Another idea was to stand at the intersection of Yonge and Dundas as four garbage trucks, each one travelling at a great speed and from a different direction, crashed into him at exactly the same time. Kent also imagined freezing himself inside a block of ice and setting it beside the Henry Moore sculpture in Nathan Phillips Square. He'd do this in January. His thawing in April would be a materialization of the false promise of spring renewal.

Kent loved all these ideas, but there were problems. He couldn't figure out how to set up and secure the running chainsaws. He didn't have the money to hire four garbage trucks and their drivers. The technical knowledge needed to install a tub of water in front of city hall was beyond him. Kent's problem wasn't creativity, but cash and expertise. He needed something simple.

Kent's mind was so preoccupied that he failed to notice the large pothole directly in his path. The front right wheel of his shopping cart fell into the hole. It tipped to the right. Kent looked down just as his empties began hitting the pavement. The sound was enormous. Quickly, Kent uprighted the cart but he used too much force and it fell to the left. The remaining bottles flew out and smashed on the road.

"*Fuck,*" Kent said. He jumped up and down. The thick soles of his workboots broke the glass into smaller pieces. "Fuck, fuck, *fucking* fuck!"

One bottle remained unbroken. Kent picked it up. He smashed it against the side of his overturned shopping cart. Then he walked back to his house, which was less than half a block away. In the coach house Kent got a broom, although he could not find a dustpan. He walked around to the front door and he went inside.

Having removed his workboots Kent continued looking

for a dustpan. He was searching the third floor when he happened to look out the window and see that his siblings were standing in the front yard.

This did not make him happy.

RICHARD, LUCY, ABBA, ANGIE and Paul stood in the grassless front yard of 465 Palmerston Boulevard. They stared at the house. They could not believe what they saw. Most of the windows were covered with cardboard. The stained glass above the doorway, which used to show the house number, had been replaced with a roughly nailed piece of plywood. Large patches of the roof were without shingles. Numerous bricks were missing from the facade and the porch leaned dangerously to the left.

"It's like it's been abandoned," Richard said.

"It's like it's been abused," Lucy said.

"It didn't used to look like this," Angie said. She turned to her left and held out her arm. Paul took a step closer to her. "Honestly. This was a beautiful house."

"Like that one," Richard said. He pointed to the house on the right, which was well kept and recently painted. All the other houses on Palmerston Boulevard were. Theirs was the only one that wasn't.

"The neighbours must just hate him," Abba said. Then

she walked up the steps and onto the porch. The boards sagged under her feet. She twisted the antique doorbell. It fell into her hand. She dropped it onto the porch and the bell quietly rang.

"You don't think he still lives here?" Lucy asked.

"Oh he's in there," Richard said.

"How do you know?"

"Where else would he go?"

"There's no way he's still living here."

"Come on, Abba! Let's just go!"

"We're going in!" Abba yelled. The screen door hung on an angle. Abba pulled it open. The main door wasn't closed.

"Will you come with me?" Angie asked Paul.

"Sure," Paul said. Together they climbed the steps and went through the doorway. Abba continued to hold open the screen door. Several moments passed.

"Now!" Abba said. Lucy and Richard climbed the steps and went inside and Abba followed them in.

An even layer of grime covered everything. The chesterfield wasn't the one they remembered and this one had the legs sawn off of it. The bulbs in the chandelier had been replaced with candles. Black soot stained the wall above the fireplace. But much more disturbing were the things that hadn't changed. Angie saw her winter coat hanging in the front hall closet. Her basketball was on the shelf above it. Their family portrait still hung on the wall. The room had the feel of a shipwreck, one that had sunk quickly, without warning.

They were still in the hallway when Kent came down the stairs. His hair and his beard were long. His feet were bare. His toenails were yellow. He looked like a mountain man and he reeked of stale booze. Six or seven steps from the bottom, Kent stopped. His eyes became wide and he gripped the banister tightly.

"Kent?" Abba said. "It's me. It's us!"

"You . . . *fuckers*!" Kent screamed. They took a step back. Kent remained on the stairs. He kicked the wall with his bare foot. Large pieces of plaster fell onto the steps.

"You *fucking* fuckers. You *fucking* think you can come back? Just like this? You can just return? *Fuck* you! You fucking *fuckers*!"

Even Abba turned and ran. No one looked back until they had safely reassembled in the grassless front yard. They listened to the sound of Kent breaking things and occasionally screaming the word *fuck*.

"What do you think he could be breaking?"

"It didn't look like there was that much stuff to break."

"Maybe he's re-breaking things," Angie said. She stepped closer to Paul and then she leaned into his shoulder and he put his arm around her. For a moment it was quiet inside the house. Then a series of objects—a baseball glove, a comic book and several dresses—were thrown from the top left window on the second floor.

"That's my room," Angie said. She pointed to a window that several volumes of the Encyclopaedia Britannica were flying out of. The books landed on the sloped roof of the porch and slowly slid down. Angie took Paul's hand and put it on top of her stomach. A board game sailed through the window. The fake money scattered into the air and then it rained down on top of them, like confetti.

BOOK TWO:

Triple Terror

THREE HOURS AFTER THEY'D learned of their father's accident Richard was left in charge while their mother accompanied the police to the station. It seemed there were some questions. Why the Shark chose to go with her, and not stay with them, they did not know. They didn't even think to ask. They sat in the living room in a state of shock, not knowing what to do. Richard looked at his watch. He waited for ten minutes to pass and then he looked at it again. Only one minute had.

"I have no idea what we should be doing," Richard said.

Kent was the only one who sat on the floor. He had been given the game ball, which he threw up into the air and caught. "We should unpack Rainytown," he said.

"That feels very wrong to me," Abba said.

"No," Richard said, "it's perfect."

The cottage had been sold a year and a half earlier and Rainytown had been flattened and stored in the attic. Richard led the way. The rest of them followed him up. It did not take them long to reassemble it. They didn't try to make it sturdy. Instead they focused on putting everything back in the right place, making all of it like it used to be.

In twenty minutes it was done. They all stood in front of it. And then Richard turned around and faced them.

"I propose," he said, "that Rainytown needs a cemetery."

"I think it should go right there," Lucy said and she pointed to the Greet Your Meat Stockyards.

"I agree," Angie said. Kent was already heading downstairs for supplies, but Abba blocked his way.

"I won't have anything to do with this," Abba said.

Kent pushed past her. He returned with glue and paper and scissors and pencil crayons. The four of them got to work. Several sheets of green construction paper became the grass. The tombstone was cut from a black shoebox. With a white pencil crayon Richard began to write on it.

"Wait," Abba called. She'd been so quiet that they'd forgotten she was there. "At least use a question mark."

"I think I'd kinda like that," Angie said.

Richard looked at Kent and Lucy. They didn't disagree. It was an idea that, at the time, presented a small measure of relief. Richard handed the pencil crayon to Abba and in thick block capitals she wrote:

BESNARD RICHARD WEIRD
JANUARY 22ND, 1960–?

Abba set the tombstone inside the Rainytown Bone Orchard. It was the only one. They didn't make any more. Not then, not ever. Lucy crafted tiny paper flowers and put them on the grave. They had a moment of silence. Then they all breathed out at once. They felt strong enough to go back downstairs and wait for their mother to come home.

No one made dinner. Nine o'clock came and their mother wasn't home. Then it was ten and she still wasn't there. Just before midnight Richard turned on the television.

"*Triple Terror*," he said.

Every fourth Friday Cable 57 aired a show called *Triple Terror*. Starting at midnight they'd play three monster movies back to back to back. Under normal conditions the Weird children would wait until their mom and dad were sound asleep and then they'd all creep downstairs. They'd sit close to the TV and keep the volume low. They'd watch all three movies. Anyone falling asleep would be punched awake. They loved it if the movie was black and white. They loved it even more when you could see the strings on the flying saucers. But the ones they loved the most were the movies where the monster was obviously a man in a costume.

The night of their father's accident they watched all three movies. None of them fell asleep. After the monster movies they watched an infomercial and then the national anthem played and then the station began to broadcast a test pattern. They muted the television but they did not turn it off. They fell asleep, together, on the couches.

When they woke up the next morning, their mother and grandmother still weren't home.

RICHARD, LUCY, ABBA, ANGIE and Paul stood on the lawn, looking up. After the board games came dishware. Then record albums. Then dress shoes. Once the siblings and Paul retreated to the sidewalk objects ceased being chucked from Angie's former bedroom window. They all stood at the end of the driveway, staring at the dilapidated house.

They had failed to anticipate that both the house and Kent would have slipped into such disrepair.

"Where are we going to sleep?" Angie asked.

"Can't we get a hotel?" Paul said.

"That's so New York, Sir Spendalot," Lucy said.

"Hey," Angie said to Paul. "They're treating you like family!"

"If we leave the property, so will Kent," Richard said.

"And we'll never see him again," Abba said.

"Then maybe Paul and I can go?" Angie asked.

"That's not fair."

"Agreed."

"If one of us has to stay, we all have to stay."

"But I'm pregnant!"

"That is really getting old, Angie."

"What about the camping stuff?" Abba asked.

"Do you think it's still there?" Angie asked.

"Maybe Kent sold it," Lucy said.

"Or gave it away," Abba said.

"It's a pretty safe bet that Kent hasn't used it," Richard said.

In the mid-nineties Besnard had impulsively purchased camping equipment with the hopes of making them a tighter family unit. The gear had never been used. After several weeks of sitting in the front hallway, the equipment had been stored in the attic of the coach house. Which is exactly where they found it, perfectly preserved. There was a Coleman stove, a large cooler and three tents. Lucy and Abba shared one. Paul and Angie were given the second and Richard got one to himself.

It was a perfect one-night solution. However, Kent showed no signs of venturing out, and so his siblings spent the next five days roughing it in the grassless backyard of Palmerston Boulevard. Taking shifts, one of them guarded the front door while another watched the back. This was done twenty-four hours a day. Those not standing guard were free to do as they pleased. Which turned into sitting around the picnic table in the backyard, drinking wine and playing cards. Except for the fact that their father was dead, their mother was institutionalized and their youngest brother occasionally threw objects at them from above, they were finally having the camping experience that Besnard had always envisioned.

But four nights spent sleeping on an air mattress was all Angie's pregnant body could take. On April 16, four days before Grandmother Weird's birthday, she commandeered the coach house and sent Paul to IKEA to buy a bed. Just after 3:00 p.m., as afternoon sunlight flooded into the coach house, she sat on the floor and watched Paul as he struggled to assemble a white Leirvik bedframe.

"Jesus fuck! Goddamn it!" he yelled as he tried to interpret the pictograms.

Angie watched him for a while and then she lay down on the floor, but her view of the ceiling only encouraged her nostalgia. When she and her sisters were teenagers, making curfew had been extremely important to their father. Dates were to be concluded, promptly, at 11:00 p.m. on the front steps. Besnard was extremely inflexible on this, which was why, twenty to forty minutes before eleven o'clock, depending on the skills of whom they were dating, they'd sneak into the coach house. This way, no matter how hot and heavy things got they'd still be home on time—the coach house's proximity to the front door turned it into a sort of teenage love motel. It was where each of the three Weird daughters had lost her virginity.

"Jesus! What the fuck do they . . . Christ! It makes no sense! Wait. Damn it!" Paul said. Angie watched him take off his shirt. His back was sweaty. His profanities were ludicrously similar to the ones Zach had uttered to her during foreplay. She waited until he'd finished assembling the bed. Then she stood and ran across the room as quickly as she could. Colliding, they fell backwards. The bed sagged but it held.

"I love you," Angie said. She started unbuttoning things.

"What about the baby?"

"She loves you too. I think you'll have to take me from behind."

"I can do that."

Afterwards they lay on their backs, smiling, relaxed and believing in life. "Listen, I gotta tell you something," Paul said. "I got a call last week. From the Hendersons?"

"No. Don't do this."

"So you did contact them?"

"We're having such a beautiful moment."

"They said you were talking to them about adoption? Is that right?"

"Let's just have this. Let's just be in the moment. This moment. Please?"

"They seemed to believe that you were pretty keen about it. In fact they were surprised to hear that I didn't know," Paul said. He raised his eyebrows. She knew that he was waiting, patiently but not without a limit, for her to explain herself.

"Listen. I had coffee with them. That's it. That's all. I didn't agree to anything. If they thought I had, well that's just them being overeager."

"Wait. So without me, you met with . . . this is . . . that is too far!"

"Paul, it's just such a big commitment for me. For us! Are you really ready?"

"Yes! Yes I am! I'm so ready for this. Aren't you?"

Angie did not have an answer to this. At least not one she wanted to speak aloud. Paul believed her reluctance to commit was due to a lack of love. But the opposite was true. The amount of love she felt for both him and their unborn daughter terrified her. She feared that raising this child, with him, would generate so much love that it would simply sweep her away. Just like her mom had been swept away.

Angie closed her eyes. When she opened them again Paul was still staring at her. His teeth remained set. He turned his head slightly to the left and he kept on looking at her. This is why Angie was filled with relief when the door burst open and her siblings rushed in.

"He's rounding third!"

"Don't be stupid. He's obviously already earned a run!"

"Eight and half months ago . . ."

"Nice girth."

"We're gonna talk about this later," Paul said. Ignoring them he continued to stare at Angie.

"But really Paul, an anchor tattoo? Isn't that a little too clichéd? Even as irony?"

"Thank God we weren't twenty minutes earlier."

"More like ten."

"Five!"

"Angie, I'm serious. We're gonna talk about this later."

"I've always wondered if keeping the cap is worth the maintenance."

"Here," Abba said. She tossed the white cotton sheet that they hadn't had a chance to use. Paul had just covered them as Lucy, Abba and Richard climbed onto the bed.

"Careful," Paul said, "it's IKEA."

"Why are you here?"

"Richard says it's time."

"It's time," Richard said.

"How do you know?"

"I just know," Richard said. "It's safe. Or at least as safe as it's ever going to be."

THEY STOOD ON THE PORCH and no one moved, or spoke, not even Abba.

"Why do I get the feeling that this is a bad idea?" Richard finally asked.

"We'll all be fine," Abba answered.

"Do you know for certain that we'll be fine or are you just hoping that we'll be fine?"

"It's just Kent!" Abba said. Her voice was queenly. She opened the door and held it open. A pause, and then, "Don't be assholes!"

The queen had vanished, leaving only their sister Abba. In the end, it was the latter who had more pull and so they followed her inside. Angie was the last one in and she let the screen door slam behind her, something she'd been doing since she was twelve.

"Are you ever going to stop doing that?" Richard asked, loudly.

"Jesus!" Lucy yelled. Abba, who had pressed her hands over her ears, nodded in agreement.

"You weren't raised in a *fucking* barn," a voice screamed from the top of the staircase. This was a phrase often uttered by their father. Hearing it said in a voice so like his spooked them all.

"Sorry," Angie said.

"You guys sure waited long enough," Kent called down.

"We didn't know that throwing things was a formal invitation," Lucy said.

"How's this? Come the *fuck* up. There's something I want to show you."

"Where are you?"

"Upstairs!"

"Upstairs or up-upstairs?"

"Up-upstairs. And take your shoes off."

"Really?" Angie asked. She examined the floor. It seemed more threatening to her socks than her shoes were to it. "You can't be serious."

"Take off your shoes!"

"We're doing it," Abba said. She bent over and started unlacing. None of the rest of them moved.

"What do you think he wants?" Angie whispered.

"I don't think he wants to do anything unforetold," Abba said.

"What are you? From the nineteenth century?" Lucy asked. "Who talks like that?"

"I'm with Abba on this one," Richard said. "I think he just wants us to go up and see him. I do think we should take our shoes off though."

"I want a special exemption," Angie said.

"No exemptions," Richard said. "But sit down and I'll help you."

Angie sat down on the third stair from the bottom. She held out her feet and caught Lucy's eye. "See?" she told her. "That's a sibling who cares."

When they were all shoeless Richard put his hand on the banister. He paused, briefly. Then he began climbing the stairs. They followed him up. On the second floor landing Richard brushed his hand on his pants. He continued up to the third floor without putting it back on the railing. The window at the top of the stairs was covered with cardboard. It seemed that all of the windows were covered with something. They stood, close together, in complete darkness.

"Angie, get the light," Richard said.

"No way," she said. "Absolutely no way."

The light switch on the third floor had always been political. It wasn't at the top of the stairs, but on the wall across from the top of the stairs. Turning it on required two steps in complete darkness and then groping blindly along the wall until the switch was located. It was a task that had always fallen to Angie.

"Why should I do it?" Angie asked.

"Because you always did it," Lucy said.

"But I'm pregnant."

"Not our fault."

"You gotta let that go."

"Already old."

"Vote," Lucy suggested.

"I can't even see who's voting."

"Angie, just do it."

"There's probably no power anyway."

"This is so unfair."

"Truth isn't fair."

"What does making me turn on a light switch have to do with truth?"

"Just get the switch," Richard said.

Angie knew it was no use fighting them. She held the banister. She put her left foot directly against the post. She took two steps into the darkness. When she touched the wall Angie ran her hand up and down until she felt the switch.

"Such a stupid place for a light switch," Angie said. She flicked it. The hall light failed to come on but a flame burst in front of her face. The flame lit a candle and revealed the face of Kent. The full drifter-style beard made him almost unrecognizable and the candle lit him from underneath, giving his face a ghoulish quality.

"Why do you have a phone number on your forearm?" he asked.

"No hello? No good-to-see-you-after-eight-years? Or oh-my-God-you're-pregnant?"

"Those things are explainable."

"The Shark did it."

"See? Now I understand. Why did she . . . never mind. That can wait. How are they?" Kent said and he nodded towards the rest of his siblings who remained huddled at the top of the steps.

"About the same."

"That's too bad."

"Abba's with us."

"I know."

"How are you? I mean, are you okay?"

"Who's the new guy?"

"He's the dad."

"Let's hope he'll be better than ours."

"He already is," she said.

"May I?" he asked. He pointed to her stomach. Angie nodded. Kent passed her the candle and then he put both of his palms on her belly. She had been waiting for one of them to do this.

"Don't cry."

"I' . . . m . . . not."

Kent kept his hands on Angie's stomach for several moments more. They were still there when Richard, Abba, Lucy and Paul moved behind her.

"I'm glad it's you that reproduced," Kent said.

"Well I haven't done it yet," she said. She knocked on the wooden door frame. Kent removed his hands and then took three giant backwards steps. He raised his arms over his head. With his left foot he kicked the door of what had been his bedroom. It swung open. A flickering yellow glow spilled out. Bowing low, Kent beckoned them inside.

Only Abba accepted the invitation. They watched her disappear into his bedroom. Then she gasped so loudly that they rushed and struggled to get inside.

Collectively, as a herd of Weirds, they ran towards Kent's room. None of them knew for certain whether Abba's gasp had been provoked by joy or fear. Kent had spent years living like a squatter, being homeless in his own home, and they had no idea what he was capable of—or what he'd created in there.

Angie was last inside. Seeing it stopped her cold. Then she started to sob.

"Crybaby," Kent whispered.

Kent had rebuilt Rainytown. Their cardboard city stretched between all four walls of his old room. But he had done so much more than simply set up the houses and the buildings. Using clear tape he'd repaired every tear in every piece of cardboard. He'd reinforced the larger multi-storey buildings with popsicle sticks. For the interior of Abba's castle he'd used chopsticks and duct tape.

Every building had been repainted and not one of them was a shade away from its original colour, even the pink on Abba's castle. The lettering on the signs had been darkened and redrawn but Kent had been able to keep the original handwriting. The sign above the Endoh World Laundry-Matt was still recognizably Abba's. The Terminal Bus Terminal was still in Richard's thirteen-year-old scrawl.

He'd added things too. The most obvious was that he'd run electricity into town. Tiny proportionally sized lamp-posts ran down both sides of every street. The lights were on inside every building that would have been open after dark. So a yellow glow came out of The Stake House, the only restaurant in Rainytown catering to the vampire population. It was also on in The Hanging Garden, where at the end of every meal the customers were not served with a check, but a noose. Yet Dr. U. Vernt Goodenough's Plastic Surgery Palace, The Cut Brakes Used Car Lot, and Styx and Stoners Used Musical Instruments were dark.

"Is it perfect?" Kent asked.

It took Angie a second to understand that he was talking to her. She was still noticing details, like the black pipe cleaners he'd used to twist their family name into the front gate of the Rainytown Bone Orchard. And how the paper flowers on their father's grave were fresh.

"Yes. It is," Angie said.

"It really is," Richard said.

"Better than before," Abba said.

"Much better," Lucy said.

"Good," Kent said. He raised his hands above his head. He opened and closed his fingers as if they were claws.

Then he took one big awkward Godzilla-like step towards Rainytown.

"No! Kent! Don't!" Angie yelled.

At the very edge of Rainytown, his foot raised in the air, Kent stopped. He looked up at the ceiling. "Rwarrrrrrr," Kent screamed. The word he'd used was at best a pale imitation of a sound remembered from the monster movies they'd watched so long ago. Yet it conveyed so much pain and sadness and anger that none of them could imagine a better one. It said everything they were feeling. What none of them had ever figured out how to express. Kent stepped forwards and he stomped on the water tower, grinding it into the floor as if he were extinguishing a cigarette.

Richard did not hesitate. He screamed and raised his hands over his head and took out most of Maimstreet with one sweeping kick. Abba went straight for the castle, pulling it down with her teeth and then spitting out its paper foundation. Lucy worked her way up Blood & Guts Boulevard, hopping on top of one building and then the next. Stopping his path of destruction Kent looked over his shoulder at Angie.

"Rwarr?" he asked, tenderly.

"Rwarr," she repeated. Holding her stomach she stepped forwards and destroyed the cemetery with a single kick of her socked foot. They continued jumping and tearing and screaming.

Within minutes, Rainytown lay in ruins.

BOOK THREE:

The Theory of Snakes and Sharks

As the automatic doors to Lester B. Pearson International Airport slid open, the Weirds—plus Paul—had done what they could. They'd spent the day before packing and buying tickets and trying to get cleaned up. Kent's hair and beard had been trimmed and they'd bought him new clothes. Lucy's and Angie's mom-made haircuts were tucked under woollen caps. Richard bought the tickets online with his platinum card and at the check-in counter he did all the talking. The six of them received their boarding passes and checked their luggage without incident.

They passed through security without a frisk or an alarm. In the designated waiting area beside Gate 23 they waited for twenty-six minutes. Then flight AC808 from Toronto to Vancouver began to board.

Their strategy was to put those they anticipated causing the most problems at the front. The hope was that the weight of suspicion wouldn't accumulate until the sketchiest of them was already on board. Kent went first. He showed his boarding pass. The flight attendant didn't notice that his driver's licence was expired. He was waved ahead. At the back of the line Angie tried not to look too relieved.

The flight attendant commented on how much she liked Lucy's hat. She gave Abba a respectful nod, and she did not question her Uplifftian passport. Richard was sent forwards with a flirtatious smile. In Angie's mind the worst was over. With Paul behind her, she stepped forwards and presented her boarding pass. The flight attendant looked her over. First her eyes rested on the phone number on her forearm. Then they lowered to her stomach.

"Do you have a note?" the flight attendant asked. She chewed her gum. She blew a small pink bubble, which broke.

"I have my boarding pass."

"From your doctor."

"I'm not sick."

"How many weeks along are you?"

"Let's call it thirty-six. She's a kicker."

"Sorry," said the flight attendant. She obviously wasn't. Seeing an opportunity to exercise the scant authority she'd been endowed with, she continued. "I can't let you fly. We can't let anyone beyond thirty-five weeks board."

"Oh. Sorry, then. I simply made a mistake. I'm only thirty-four weeks along."

"Can you prove it?"

"Excuse me?" Angie asked the flight attendant. "I've boarded several flights just this week."

"The safety and security of *all* passengers on board is one of my chief responsibilities."

"What are you talking about?"

"Don't do it," Paul whispered into Angie's ear.

"I'm sorry, those are the rules," the flight attendant said.

There are several explanations for what Angie said next. She had not slept well in many days. There were hormones racing through her body. She was literally inches away from achieving an impossible goal. But in truth, Angie simply couldn't believe that a come-to-life self-righteous Barbie had this much power over her. The woman's hair was too perfectly pulled into a bun. Her feet did not seem pinched in her high heels, which caused her no effort to stand in. Her white blouse had that one extra button open. The very tilt of her head said that this job was just something she was doing until someone rich made her his wife. And the height that her bra lifted her boobs made it clear that she wouldn't be waiting long.

"My dear girl . . ." Angie said.

"Just don't do it," Paul repeated.

Angie stopped. She regained her composure. The flight attendant blew yet another bubble. When it popped so did Angie. "Don't be such a cunt!" Angie yelled, emphasizing the *t*.

The flight attendant was speechless. A full second passed in which she did not react at all. Then she held up Angie's boarding pass and ripped it in two. She tore the halves into quarters. She let the pieces fall from her hands. Angie watched the white paper squares flutter to the floor. And then, from the corner of her eye, she saw Kent rushing towards them.

Two security guards tackled Kent before he even got close. His face hit the carpet. His lip burst open. Blood landed on the collar of his clean white shirt. The taller guard pressed a knee into the small of Kent's back. The other one forced Kent's arms behind him. At no time did Kent resist.

"You let him go!" Abba screamed.

"He's done nothing wrong!" Richard yelled.

"Right now! Let him go right now!" Lucy yelled.

The guard put his giant right hand on the back of Kent's head. Yet Kent easily looked up at Angie. The fabric of his shirt outlined the muscles in his arms. He started to stand, taking both guards with him.

"Don't, Kent," Angie said "I'm so sorry. Please don't make it worse." Kent looked at Angie. "Please?"

Kent nodded and then he lowered himself back to the carpet. The guards were confused. Then they quickly secured Kent's hands behind his back.

Angie turned to the flight attendant. "I'm so sorry," she said. "We'll just leave. All of us."

The security guards were happy to have Kent. They nodded their consent and the flight attendant acquiesced. Angie touched Lucy and Abba on the shoulder. She took Richard by the hand. Paul followed as they left Kent behind.

———

For three hours they stood on the sidewalk in front of Lester B. Pearson International Airport. Planes flew overhead. Angie watched vapour trails criss-cross and dissolve. Just after noon she looked back at her family. Abba sat on the sidewalk with her hands folded in her lap. Lucy's eyes were red-rimmed. Paul hovered several steps behind, as if awaiting instructions. Richard stood by himself, to the right, with a cigarette in his mouth and a Zippo in his hand, both of which were unlit. To Angie they looked like a painting in the Renaissance style. And then Kent walked into it.

Kent stood so perfectly between Lucy and Richard that his appearance didn't demand attention. It completed the picture. The two guards who'd escorted him stepped into the background. Kent took the lighter from Richard's hand. He brushed it against his jeans. He held the flame to the end of the cigarette. Richard exhaled before he realized how odd this was.

"Jesus!" Richard said.

"It's like, what, two days? Two days and a bit?" Kent asked. He capped the Zippo and handed it back to Richard. "If the Shark's not kicking until the twentieth and we drive it in shifts, really fast, we can make it."

"He could be right," Angie said.

"We'll just rent a car!" Lucy said. She was too impressed by Kent's idea to be surprised by his presence.

"A van!"

"Why do you people always doubt me?"

"Because you haven't brushed your teeth in eight years?"

"You just saw me do it!"

"And before that?"

"Be nice to Kent," Angie said. "I think he just saved us."

"Fifty-one hours and fifty-four minutes, according to MapQuest," Richard said, reading from his phone. "So, ya. We can make it."

"Where's a car rental place?"

"They're inside," Angie said.

The security guards remained by the doors. Angie raised her hand. A taxi pulled in front of them. The trunk popped open and she put her carry-on inside it.

"Not this one. There's a dent on the side," Lucy said.

"We are in no position to be choosy," Angie said.

"The dent merely mirrors our current situation," Richard said.

"What about the rest of our luggage?" Abba asked.

"Don't be so attached to material things," Kent said.

"Shut up, Kent," Lucy said.

"Just because you're too poor to have material things doesn't make you holy," Abba said.

"We can buy new stuff when we get there," Angie said.

"Shotgun!" Kent called, and no one challenged him.

At 2:35 p.m., having rented a white Ford Econoline van from Discount Car and Truck Rentals, they began driving west. The interior was grey and it had two bench seats.

Angie and Paul sat in the middle. Lucy and Abba sat behind them. Richard drove and Kent retained shotgun. Twenty minutes passed and then, with the needle still pointing above the F, having just agreed that they would stop only for food and gas, Angie felt a desperate need to pee.

"I need to pee," she told them. "Desperately."

The van did not slow. Neither Richard nor Kent took their eyes from the road.

"I'm sorry. I'm really sorry. But I need to pee."

Richard's foot kept the gas pedal depressed. Kent turned around in the passenger seat. "Can't you just hold it?" he asked her.

"I'm eight and a half months pregnant!"

"Which is why we had to rent this van."

"That does not change the fact that I really need to pee."

"Since you were six!" Abba called from the back row.

"You get in a car and you think you need to pee!" Lucy said. "It's in your head!"

"It's in my uterus! On top of my bladder!"

"Vote," Kent called.

"A vote will not change how desperately I need to pee."

"All for stopping?" Richard called. He looked through the rear-view mirror. Angie's and Paul's were the only hands that were raised.

"And against?" Richard asked. The rest of Angie's siblings put up their hands.

"The nays have it."

"I'm going to pee my pants and then the whole van will smell like pee . . ."

"No you won't."

"Just hold it!"

"Don't be such a suck."

". . . smelly pregnant-woman pee!"

"To pull over now would be a repudiation of democracy. Is that what you want?"

"Angie's a commie!"

"Pull this goddamn van over right now!" Paul said. Having grown up with six sisters, Paul's vocal skills were estimable. His version of *the Tone*, while not quite as powerful as the Shark's, was more than persuasive enough. "Right now," Paul repeated, quietly.

"Okay, okay," Richard said. "Where?"

"Right here!"

"Here?"

"Good enough."

The van slowed. Richard let a white Honda Civic pass on the right and then he pulled onto the unpaved shoulder. Angie slid the van door open and jumped out. She stood at the side of the road. There were no bushes or trees. The grass had been recently mowed. Cars and eighteen-wheelers zoomed behind her.

"Damn it," Angie said. Then she turned around and she saw Paul climb out of the van. He held his jacket by the shoulders, turning it into a curtain. With little choice and less time Angie squatted. Several moments passed before either of them spoke.

"You really have a lot in there," Paul said.

"Try not to think about it."

"I love you."

"Jesus, Paul. Not now."

"We're gonna make great parents."

"No, fuck, Paul. No, we are not."

"I'm sorry. It's just . . ."

"Find me some toilet paper!"

"Okay."

"Now! Right now!"

"Okay," Paul repeated. He wrapped his jacket around her shoulders. Angie continued to squat by the side of the road. She held his coat by the lapels. She waited until Paul was back inside the van and then she pressed her face against the fabric and she breathed in deeply.

BESNARD WEIRD, IN THE YEARS preceding his sudden absence, had many possessions but only one that was sacred: his maroon 1947 Maserati A6 Pininfarina Berlinetta. Besides him, only his daughters had ever driven it. On each of these occasions, the car had been damaged.

Lucy was the first to drive it. Although it had taken her days, she'd mustered the nerve both to ask her father for the keys and Angus Kieffer out on a date. She'd been surprised when both had said yes. She returned Angus unharmed, but her father's car had suffered a minuscule ding in the right door. Besnard easily found this almost invisible mark and forbade her from ever driving the car again.

Six days after her sixteenth birthday Abba took the keys from her father's bedside table and then went on a drive into the country. When she returned the car was without its right side-view mirror. How this happened, she never explained.

———

Angie was the last of the Weird daughters to drive the Maserati. She found the keys in the right front pocket of a pair of her father's navy-blue dress pants. In this same pocket she also found a tube of lipstick, cherry red. This was a shade her mother would have found crass. While by no means irrefutable evidence of adultery, Angie knew. She just knew.

She left the lipstick but took the keys. Backing out of the coach house she struck a telephone pole at considerable speed. The left tail light burst into a million tiny pieces.

Because of these accidents, the boys never got a chance to drive the car. But much more cruel, at least from their teenage perspectives, was that Besnard never fixed any of the damage his daughters had caused. He did not remove the dent from the door. He didn't replace the side-view mirror or the shattered tail light. He left all three as visual reminders that his authority wasn't arbitrary. That it existed for reasons of protection, which should never be questioned.

The siblings just thought he was being an asshole. Except Angie, of course, who forgave him, instantly.

Here's something else that Angie did her best never to think about: she was the last person to talk to their father. It was shortly before eleven on November 22, 2001. She and Zach had just rushed out of the coach house. They made it to the porch at 10:57 p.m. But the front door was closed. The porch light was off and her father wasn't there.

Angie gave Zach a peck on the cheek and said goodnight. She went inside. "Dad?" she called. There was no answer. She knew that her mother, Abba and Lucy had gone to a play. Richard was at his girlfriend's. Kent was likely up in his room, doing something she didn't want to know about. The house was silent. If it hadn't been, she would never have heard the garage door of the coach house being pulled open.

Angie panicked. Believing that her father had seen her out there with Zach she became filled with anxiety. This grew into dread, which became so heavy that she decided to get it over with as quickly as she could. She went out to the coach house and found her father unlocking the driver's side door of the station wagon.

"Where are you going?" she asked him.

"It's . . ." he said, looking down, "a work thing."

"You're taking the wagon?" she asked.

Besnard hated the station wagon. He did not like being seen in it. When the whole family had to go somewhere all at once, he sometimes agreed to sit in the passenger seat. But more often he'd follow behind in the Maserati. "Oh. Ya. Right," he said. He gave a small embarrassed laugh. He moved away from the station wagon and unlocked the Maserati. He opened the driver's side door and then he looked at her. "You know," he said. He paused.

He flicked through his keys one at a time. "I love you."

This was the first time he'd ever told her this. It would also be the last thing he ever said to her.

TEN HOURS OUT OF TORONTO, seven from Thunder Bay and seventeen from Winnipeg, Angie flicked on her low beams as the first car they'd met in sixty minutes drove past. She watched its tail lights fade in the rear-view mirror. She turned the high beams back on and tried to imagine what life would be like without her blursing, but the only thing illuminated was the landscape.

Needing time alone—or as close to it as she could get—Angie had volunteered to do the overnight shift. The baby usually kept her awake during those hours anyway. But the drive hadn't been solitary. While the others slept, Abba and Lucy continued a conversation they'd been having since the radio had lost all reception.

"But . . . as queen, specifically, what is required of you?" Lucy asked.

"There are a lot of official functions. Ceremonies, that sort of thing," Abba answered.

"Do you attend Parliament? Do you sign things into law?"

"No. The king did that."

"Exactly. Okay. But after he died . . . he passed in 2007?"

"That's right."

"Who took over that sort of thing?"

"What are you trying to get at?" Abba asked. Lucy did not immediately answer. The pause was long enough that all three of them noticed the car. It came up behind them, quickly. Then it was beside them. There it stayed for five or six seconds before it sped off. With so few cars on the road it would have caught their attention even if it hadn't been a red Maserati.

"What ever happened to Dad's car?" Abba asked.

"I don't know. I really don't know," Angie said.

"I don't remember seeing it in the coach house," Lucy said.

"It wasn't there. I would have seen it getting the camping stuff."

"Or when we built the bed."

"But it wasn't in the driveway either."

"Maybe Kent sold it?" Abba asked.

The probability of Kent arranging and negotiating this sale, let alone permitting it, was so low that they felt no need to wake him. Plus, he was still *fucking* mad that they'd unanimously voted against letting him drive. The Maserati pulled farther away. Angie stepped on the gas.

"The left tail light's missing," Abba said.

"I noticed that too."

"Was it the left or the right?"

"It was the left," Angie said.

"Are you sure?"

"Absolutely."

"What about the side-view?"

"It's too dark to tell."

"Then get closer," Abba said.

The needle pointed to 120 km/h. Angie further depressed the gas pedal. The engine began to make a high-pitched whine. The single red tail light got farther away.

"Angie, don't be chicken-shit!"

"Catch up to it!"

"I'm trying," she said. The tail light continued to recede. Angie drove faster still. The whine got louder. It got higher in pitch. Then the tail light disappeared.

"Where'd he go?"

"I don't know! I don't know!"

"The turnoff," Lucy shouted, pointing. "The turnoff!"

Angie steered sharply to the right. She tried to slow down. As she hit the off-ramp at 90 km/h, the van began to tilt. Angie braked. They came to a sudden stop. Their bodies were thrown forwards and then jarred back. This woke everyone up.

No one said anything. Beside them was a stop sign. On top of it was a flashing red light. The inside of the van glowed red. Then it didn't. And then it did again.

"There it is," Abba said and she pointed to the right. A single red tail light sped away. They watched it until they couldn't see it. In the passenger seat Paul turned and looked at Angie. His face was red and then it wasn't and then it was again.

"Are you okay?" Paul asked.

"Where are we?" Richard asked.

"What the *fuck* is going on?"

"We're chasing ghosts," Lucy said. Abba and Angie could only nod their heads in agreement.

W

AT 4:30 P.M., THE AFTERNOON AFTER they'd chased the Maserati, having finally crossed the Ontario/Manitoba border and started over the Prairies, the sun was neither golden nor setting as Lucy pulled in front of the Golden Sunsets Retirement Community. From the middle bench Angie looked in the rear-view mirror. Lucy was already looking at her.

"I don't think we have time for this," Angie said, quietly.

"It's about time. It's About Time," Lucy answered. She did not look away until Angie did. The driver's door opened. Then it slammed closed, waking everybody else up.

"Where are we?" Kent asked. "Why did we stop?"

"I believe," Richard said, looking out the window and recognizing the building from the brochure, "we're at Winnipeg's fourth best retirement community."

They all got out of the van. When Paul did too, Angie stopped him. "Please stay here?" she asked.

"What? No. I want to meet your mother."

"No you don't."

"Yes I do!"

"I don't want you to," she said. She saw that this hurt him. "Please?"

"Why?"

Angie looked over her shoulder. Her siblings were already inside. She didn't have enough time to make something up so she told him the truth. "I don't want you to start thinking that I'll turn into my mother. Especially now that I'm just about to become one."

"Don't worry about that. I won't."

"I'm not worried about you," she said. "I'm worried that I'll start worrying that you'll start worrying."

Paul worked through her syntax. Then he nodded. This made her love him just a little bit more. She did not say this to him.

"But soon, you know," Paul said. "She'll have to meet the baby."

"I promise," Angie said. She held her stomach and ran across the parking lot. They'd waited for her just inside the front door. Lucy led them past the grandfather clock and down the yellow hallway. They stood very close together in the elevator. Then the doors opened, revealing the handmade cardboard sign.

"Holy *fuck*."

"I'd go in but I've just had mine done," Angie said.

"Everybody goes in," Lucy said.

"I'm not going."

"Everybody goes in."

"You can't make us."

"She *fucking* doesn't even know who we are!"

"She's right," Richard said, "we're all going in." He stepped to the door of the janitor's closet and paused only briefly before he went inside.

"Do you have an appointment?" Richard heard his mother ask. His eyes were still adjusting to the dark.

"Can you fit me in?" he asked.

"Sure. It's Monday. It's slow," she said. It was Wednesday but Richard didn't correct her. As his pupils grew bigger the image of his mother developed in front of him, like a print. She had aged better than he had. She moved a chair in front of the sink and Richard sat down in it. The water was warm and she washed his hair.

"A couple of grey hairs in here," she said.

"At least."

"Are you a family man?"

"Why do you ask?"

"You seem like a family man. But there's no ring."

"I'm recently divorced," Richard said. His ring was in the front pocket of his pants. He rubbed his thumb against his finger in the space where it used to be.

"That's too bad."

"It's for the best."

"That's what your generation says. Maybe it's true. Maybe

it is for the best. Or maybe you didn't love her enough," Nicola said. She shut off the taps. She stood him up and moved the chair in front of the mirror. The peach beach towel was tied around his neck. She picked up her scissors and began cutting his hair.

"You're not going to ask me how I want it cut?"

"Are you sad?" Nicola asked. Richard turned in the chair. The scissors became motionless.

"Yes. I am sad. I'm sad most of the time."

"Does it bother you?"

"It never used to. But now it does. Very much."

"It's because the world disappoints you," Nicola said. She set down her scissors. She took a pair of electric clippers off the shelf. "It continually fails to surprise you. It fails to be as wonderful as you long for it to be. This is where your sadness comes from."

Nicola increased the setting on the shaver and turned it on. The electric hum was loud in the small room. She ran it over every inch of Richard's head. Then she turned it off. The beach towel was removed. Pieces of his hair drifted in the air around his head.

"Go ahead, look!" Nicola said.

Richard looked at his reflection. He didn't look like himself. He laughed. The skin around his eyes wrinkled into lines. These lines were deep and he had not seen them in quite some time.

"I thought you'd be open to a change," Nicola said.

"You were right," Richard said. He ran his hand over his shiny bald skull. He stood up. Clumps of hair fell from his clothes. "What do I owe you?" he asked.

"Oh, I do this for love."

"Can I hug you?"

"I don't see why not," Nicola said. She opened her arms and Richard held her tightly.

"Do you have an appointment?" Nicola asked Lucy.

"Yes. It's for now."

Nicola nodded. Lucy sat herself in the chair in front of the sink. Her mother washed her hair.

"Do you know the gentleman who was here before you?"

"Yes, I do. Quite well, in fact."

"There are many of these men in your life?"

"Oh no, it's not like that. He's my brother."

"I see," Nicola said. She rinsed out the shampoo. Lucy stood. Nicola moved the chair and tied the beach towel around her neck. She picked up her scissors but she did not begin to cut. "But there are others, no? Men, not your brothers?"

"Yes. There are."

"That you love?"

"No. Not like that. Not like you and Dad."

"Have you ever asked yourself what you're trying to give them?"

"I've never even thought about it like that."

"Because if you're trying to lose yourself, something I can't help but recommend, there are much better ways."

"But few as pleasurable."

"Well, that's true," Nicola said. They both smiled. Neither noticed that they did this in exactly the same way. "Are these affairs an attempt to figure out who you are?"

"Maybe. . ."

"And you think that everyone else already knows this? That they know who they are?"

"I do."

"You see, there, that's your mistake," Nicola said. She cut away Lucy's bangs. She cut several long lengths from the back. "As far as I can tell, you remain a mystery to yourself until the day you die."

Lucy bit her bottom lip. Nicola lifted her scissors. She set them back down. She picked up the clippers and then she turned them on.

It is perhaps unfair to attribute Abba's anger solely to a fear of losing her long red hair. She stormed into the janitor's closet with her hands in fists. "Enough, Mother," Abba said. "Enough!"

"It's been a busy morning. But I'm sure I can fit you in."

"Stop it! Mother?"

"You have gorgeous hair."

"Just come back to us."

"It's so long."

"This could be the last chance."

"It's most unusual. This length. Don't you think?"

"I need you. We all do."

"Maybe it's just for beauty," Nicola said. She reached out her hand and ran it through Abba's hair. "But maybe not? Let's just give it a wash?"

Abba's fingers uncurled. She sat down in the chair in front of the sink. The smell of the goat's milk shampoo and the warmth of the water made her feel safe. This feeling remained as she sat in front of the mirror. Nicola tied the towel around her neck. Then she handed her the scissors.

"Maybe you want to make the first cut?" Nicola asked.

Abba looked at the scissors. She looked at them for quite some time. Then she pulled out a length of her hair, put the scissors quite close to her scalp and she cut. Abba kept this lock of hair in her hand as she passed the scissors back to her mother. She was still holding it when Nicola turned off the clippers.

Angie, her hair wet, sat in front of the mirror. The beach towel was already tied around her neck. Nicola put her hands on her daughter's shoulders. She pressed down, hard. Through the mirror Nicola looked into Angie's eyes. "You know, you're very strong," Nicola said.

"Thank you."

"That's no compliment. It's your weakness. If you weren't so strong you wouldn't have to take it and so you wouldn't," she said. Then she lifted her hands and took up her scissors and she began to cut. Angie looked down. She thought about what her mother had just said. She was still preoccupied with these thoughts when she realized that the annoying buzz was the sound of an electric shaver.

"No! Wait!" she called. But Nicola had already started, so Angie just let her finish.

Kent entered the room quickly, shut the door with force and stepped towards his mother.

"Where are they?"

"Where are what?"

"The clippers. Where the *fuck* are the clippers?"

Nicola extended her index finger. She pointed to the shelf. She kept the rest of her body perfectly still. Kent crossed the room, picked up the clippers and turned them to the highest setting. With great speed and little delicacy he shaved his head. Hair fell in clumps. He turned the electric shaver off and put it back where he found it. He ran his hand over his head. It felt smooth and clean. Then it felt wet and sticky. Kent looked in the mirror and saw tiny trickles of blood flowing from several cuts over both sides of his scalp.

"Sit down," Kent heard his mother say.

Kent shook his head no.

"Let yourself be helped!" Nicola said, loudly. She pointed to the chair and Kent sat down in it. He gasped and squirmed as his mother applied alcohol and bandages to his head. But he did not verbally protest and he did not try to get out of the chair.

No one spoke as they gathered in the elevator. They rode up to the main floor. They walked through the gloomy halls. None of them returned the stares of the residents. They didn't even look at each other as they climbed back into the van.

Without anyone actually saying anything, Paul was volunteered to drive. Angie sat in the passenger seat. She let an hour's worth of prairie flatness go by before she angled the rear-view mirror. She looked at them. They all stared at the floor, occasionally running their hands over their heads. Without hair their physical similarities were frighteningly obvious; the broad noses, the high foreheads, the wrinkles at the corners of their eyes. They were, undeniably, her family and they were all together and for the first time since Grandmother Weird had written a phone number on her forearm, she felt that things were going to be okay.

THE NEXT TIME ANGIE woke up, the dashboard clock said 8:20. Her heart fell a little bit when she saw the tiny *p.m.* She looked at Paul, who reached over, lowered her visor and tapped the mirror. In it she saw her brothers in the middle row. They sat as far apart as the bench permitted. Richard started to say something. His body language indicated it was of vital importance. Then he stopped himself from saying it. And then Kent did exactly the same thing. In the two minutes Angie watched, they repeated this cycle six times.

"How long have they been doing that?" Angie whispered.

"About twenty minutes? Maybe thirty," Paul said. "Is it bad? It seems bad."

"It could blow up or over. You just never know."

The van continued forwards. The prairie continued to be flat. And then Richard picked up his camera and aimed it at Kent.

"If you take a picture of me I'll *fucking* break that thing."

"Come on."

"I'll break *you*," Kent said. Slowly he turned his head and stared at his brother. Richard lowered it to his lap. His finger remained on the shutter release button.

"You got a problem with photography?" Richard asked.

"I have several."

"Please, give us your wisdom."

"Fuck you."

"No. I'll be serious. Tell me. We have time to kill."

"Put it down."

"Put what down?"

"Put it on the floor," Kent said. The van travelled several kilometres. Then Richard took the strap from around his neck and set the camera between his feet.

"I do not like the fact that it takes the place of personal memory," Kent said. He touched his beard as if making sure it was still there. "I do not like the fact that it's become the ubiquitous documenting tool of personal history. That all other methods, specifically diaries and journals, or letter writing, or even portrait painting, are no longer deemed worthy. That now the use of photography has become so ubiquitous . . ."

"You like that word . . ."

". . . so ubiquitous that now the only accepted evidence that an event took place, that something happened, is if there are pictures of it. And, not only that, but your perception of the event is forever cemented, curated, by what the camera documents. If there are no pictures it did not happen. And if you are not in the pictures, you were not there."

"Bullshit. You can't . . ."

"May I finish?"

"Please."

"This *documentia* is now so overgrown that it no longer documents reality but creates it. Since all of our memories are now stored in these external pictures, creating a false perception that the events happened specifically as the photographs describe, we are now a nation, a species, of observers. Doomed to be spectators at the most important events of our lives. That this perspective is now so highly esteemed and unquestioned in its authority has created a means of social control more powerful than serfdom or even the Catholic Church."

"You're bringing Catholicism into this?"

"Not done."

"Sorry."

"Throughout the course of human civilization memory has been transient, plastic. The girl who broke your heart can, in time, become simply the girl you lived with ten years ago. Given more time she becomes either the one who got away or the one you can't believe you almost married. But now, in the reign of the photographic image, the past is no longer malleable. It can no longer shift meaning in order to facilitate the narrative of your present circumstances.

"We are now, all of us, cinematographers for the movie of our own lives. Not the star. Not the director. Not even the writer!"

"Well, those are very interesting—"

"But none of these reasons properly articulates why I hate not only your photographs but your use of photography in general."

"Really," Richard said. The whole car was pink and orange from a sunset that had just broken through the clouds. Angie began to worry. Her worry escalated when she noticed that Richard had started picking up the camera with his feet.

"The reason I don't like your photographs is because you use photography as a shield," Kent continued, "just like you're doing right now, Richard, and if you *fucking* reach for it, so *fucking* help me God, I'll grab Paul and force him to drive this van right into the ditch!"

"What?" asked Paul.

"It's okay," Angie said, although she wasn't sure it was. Richard froze. It remained unclear whether he was going to go for his camera or not. Then he stopped moving his feet and leaned back.

"Thank you," Kent said. "Your camera is a bubble, a semi-permeable membrane that lets in light and colour but keeps out all feeling. Every time you're in the middle of a sincere emotional moment you reach for your *fucking* camera. It's a portable cocoon. I suspect that you, dear brother, have not experienced a true emotional, honest, heartfelt moment since the day of our father's funeral."

"I think he's right," Abba said. Richard looked over his

shoulder. He realized that Abba and Lucy were listening intently.

"You do do that," Lucy said.

"Agreed," Abba said.

"How long has it been since you travelled without a camera?" Angie asked from the passenger seat.

"Stop the car!" Richard screamed.

"Don't get defensive. We're trying to help."

"Maybe you should just listen?"

"Stop the van! Seriously. Pull over. Right now. Paul—pull over!"

"Just go with it, Dick. Don't be afraid."

"Truth isn't fair."

"The right front tire is about to blow!" Richard yelled, and just as he finished saying these words, it did.

Paul struggled to keep the van under control. It veered into the right lane and only the absence of traffic prevented a collision. But Paul did not oversteer. He did not put his foot on the brake. He let the van decelerate and then he coasted onto the shoulder. They stopped, and for several seconds no one moved and then they all got out at once. Angie was the last to reach the right front tire. Lucy was kneeling down, looking at it closely, although she didn't touch it.

"It's just spooky when you do that shit, Richard," Lucy said.

"Very."

"Totally creeps me out."

"Remember that time when you predicted that Kent would break his leg if he went to hockey practice?"

"And then I went and I broke my leg!"

"You should have listened to me."

"Or maybe I broke it because you psyched me out. Maybe it never would have happened if you'd just kept your mouth shut."

"I'm hungry."

"I am too."

"Do you think that place is open?"

"It's a truck stop. Of course it is."

"We need a break."

"Totally."

"Let's go, let's go."

"Who's going to change the tire?" Richard asked.

They all stepped off the pavement. They began walking through a small field of weeds, which separated the highway from the truck stop. Not one of them looked back.

"Come on!" Richard called. He knew that in their minds predicting the blowout had made it his responsibility. And as he opened the rear doors and found the jack, part of him did not disagree. He knelt down beside the blown tire. He tried to figure out how to work the jack. He looked back at them. What he saw was perfect. In single file they walked through scrub and litter. The truck stop was their obvious destination. Two parked eighteen-wheelers defined the edges of the frame and the whole thing was lit in purple and orange.

Richard rushed back inside the van and got his camera. He found focus. He walked three steps to his right, crouched down, and focused again. His finger hovered over the shutter release.

Richard lowered his camera. He watched them walk across the field. When they were inside the truck stop he took the strap from around his neck. He set his camera on the ground. It stayed there while he changed the tire. It was still there when everyone carried food back into the van and Abba drove it away.

"Jesus Christ there it is again," Kent said.

Leaning forwards in his seat Kent watched as the Maserati passed them. Soon it was two lengths ahead of them. Its single tail light glowed in the dark. It got farther away and Kent stared at his brother.

"You're crazy," Richard said. He took his right hand off the steering wheel and ran it over his hairless head. Then he put it back. He did not increase the speed of the van.

"Why do you always doubt me?" Kent said. He punched the dashboard. It was not the sound of the hit, but the gasp of pain that followed, that woke Angie. She saw it too. Unwinding Paul's arm from her shoulder she scooched forwards on the bench. She put her face in between the driver's and passenger seat.

"You can't let it get away," Angie said. "Do not let it get away."

"You can't be serious?" Richard asked.

"Lucy and Abba and I saw it before."

"When we were in Manitoba. When you almost drove off the off-ramp!"

"Ontario. We were still in Ontario. But yes, then."

"So you're crazy too?" Richard asked.

"I just know that we saw it then and here it is again and that's weird."

"It's *fucking* getting away . . ."

Richard looked out at the highway. The single tail light had already begun to fade. He slapped his head with his open palm. He did this three more times. "This is a very bad idea," Richard said. His foot depressed the accelerator. The engine whine returned; a speed-wobble started. Both of them together woke everybody up.

"What's happening?"

"Why are we going so fast?"

"Slow down, Richard!"

Richard increased their speed. The distance between the single tail light and the van decreased. Then the red sports car was inside the beam of their headlights.

"It is a Maserati," Richard said.

"See?"

"The left tail light's out."

"Was it the left or the right? I can never remember."

"It was the left," Angie said.

"Are you sure?"

"Yes. And shut up!"

"What now?" Richard asked.

"Flash your high beams," Lucy said.

"Get closer!" Kent said.

"Don't let him get away," Abba said.

"Not this time," Angie said.

Richard flashed his high beams. He honked the horn. But the Maserati did not slow down. It didn't pull over. Richard shortened the gap between the van and the sports car. When only centimetres separated the bumpers, he veered into the left lane. He pulled alongside the car. He matched its speed. Inside the van everyone except Paul rushed to a passenger side window.

They pushed their faces against the glass. They cupped their hands around their eyes. The van raced beside the Maserati.

"Can you see him? Can you see him?" Richard asked.

Angie looked away as motion sickness set in. Richard found her eyes in the rear-view mirror.

"It's too dark," she said. "I couldn't tell."

Richard looked back to the road. His lower jaw ground against his upper one. His eyes narrowed. The van began to move faster. Angie sat down and she buckled herself in.

"What is going on?" Paul asked her.

"Put on your seat belt."

"Tell me what's happening!"

"Do it now!"

"Okay, okay," Paul said. He complied. They gained a length on the Maserati and then a second, a third and a fourth, but not a fifth.

"Not yet, Richard," Angie called. "We're still too close!"

Richard did not respond. He turned the wheel sharply to the right. He hit the brakes. Abba and Lucy were thrown to the floor. Kent crashed down on top of them. Angie heard two sets of tires squeal. She felt the van skid to a stop. She shut her eyes. When she didn't feel an impact, she opened them.

The interior of the van was quiet. Everyone was still. Then, all at once, they rushed out.

The van cut a 45-degree angle across the westbound lanes. Their headlights remained on. Dust drifted through the beams. They congregated at the centre line and stared at the Maserati. Less than six centimetres separated the two vehicles. The smell of burnt rubber was still in the air. None of them approached the Maserati. Its engine was still running. The driver stayed behind the wheel. They couldn't see his face. For several moments not one of the Weirds spoke—then they all started shouting.

"Get out of the car!"

"Right now!"

"Get out of the *fucking* car!"

"Show your face!"

"Now! Right now!"

The driver's side door began to open. The driver put his silhouetted feet onto the road. Standing up he held on to the door. He stayed behind it.

"We can't see you!"

"Turn off your lights!"

"Turn them off!"

"Show your face!"

"Now!" Angie yelled. "Right now!"

Quickly, the driver reached inside his car. He turned off his headlights. They saw how short, young and terrified he was.

"What do you want?" he asked. His voice trembled. He raised his hands over his head.

Kent turned away first. Abba, Lucy and Richard followed him. This left Angie and Paul standing on the road. Their feet straddled the centre line. Paul put his hands on her shoulders. He turned her towards the van. She was halfway there when she stopped. She looked over her shoulder at the driver, whose hands were still raised in the air.

"Your left tail light is out," she said.

For fourteen hours, as they drove through the Rocky Mountains and into British Columbia, past the most beautiful scenery in the country, no one said a word. They travelled without conversations, observations or optimism. Each of them stared out their own square of window as if the view needed to be guarded. And then, as they left the outskirts of Kamloops, they passed a sign. And the sign read:

VANCOUVER: 352

"What time is it?" Lucy asked as she drove. Her voice broke the silence so completely that no one noticed its absence.

"The clock says 7:41," Angie said, pointing to the dashboard.

"That was three time zones ago!"

"So it's . . . 4:41?"

"4:42."

"And if we drive at a hundred and twenty kilometres . . ."

"Make it a hundred and forty . . ."

"Speed limits are for *fucking* losers."

"See, Kent? Right there. That's why no one will let you drive."

"What if we hit traffic?"

"Vancouver doesn't have traffic."

"What are you talking about?"

"There was a sign. We're, like, three hundred and fifty-two kilometres away."

"Three hundred and fifty-one by now."

"How much time is that?"

"It's gonna be tight."

"Very tight."

"It may not be possible."

"But it is possible," Abba said. "We'll just go fast!"

"Agreed," Lucy said. She made the van go faster. She would not have stopped but the needle was already pointing below the E. Reluctantly she pulled into the next service station en route. Lucy jumped out and began to pump gas. Richard, Abba and Kent ran inside to get food. Paul unfastened his seat belt and he opened the door but Angie took his hand and she held it, firmly.

"I gotta go to the bathroom," he said.

"Just stay for a second."

"I really gotta go."

"This is important," Angie said. She looked at their hands and then she looked up at him.

"It can't wait?"

"Listen, we have a theory . . ."

"Who does?"

"We. The family."

"Okay?"

"It's the theory of snakes and sharks. Kent made it up. It's actually pretty complicated but the gist of it, the condensed version, is that there are two types of people who do evil in the world . . ."

"Snakes and sharks?"

"Exactly. The sharks are the people who are naturally evil. They just cruise around the world doing evil things. But that's what they do. It's in their nature. Snakes are different. They don't actually commit evil themselves, they convince other people to do it."

"Why are you telling me this?"

"The question, which we have been debating since we were little kids and which we've never been able to definitively answer is, which is worse? Is it the sharks because they are by nature evil? Or is it the snakes because they corrupt, because they bring out the evil in others? But aren't sharks just being themselves? And then again, snakes aren't technically guilty of anything. At the most they tempt others to do the things that they wanted to do in the first place."

"I'm just going to the bathroom."

"I know."

"I'll be right back."

"I know you will," Angie said. She let go of his hands.

Halfway across the parking lot Paul stopped. He looked over his shoulder. Angie waved. She smiled, broadly. She watched him until he'd gone through the men's room door.

Carrying sandwiches wrapped in plastic, Abba, Kent and Richard got into the van. As Lucy paid for the gas, Angie got into the driver's seat. She started the engine. She waited for Lucy to fasten her seat belt and then she put the van into gear. She drove onto the highway. They were seventeen minutes west of the service station before anyone noticed that the passenger seat was empty.

"Where's Paul?" Lucy asked.

"He's not a Weird," Angie said.

"He kinda is," she said. "At least, he should be."

Angie twisted the mirror until she could see Lucy in it. For several moments they looked at each other. Then Lucy nodded and she looked down and Angie turned the mirror so that no one could see her.

W

THE PASSENGER SEAT REMAINED EMPTY and Angie drove as fast as she could. She tried not to look at the clock on the dashboard. Eventually, she did. The blue digital numbers said 8:37 p.m. A very long sigh came out of her. She slowed down and pulled over.

Gravel crunched under the tires as the van came to a stop on the shoulder. Angie shifted into park, although she kept the engine running. "Is the clock still right?" she asked.

"Unfortunately," Richard said. "Three hours fast, but yes, it's keeping time."

"Then how long to Vancouver?"

"At our present speed?" asked Kent.

"Or even a little faster?" asked Abba.

"About two hours and thirty minutes," Lucy answered. "That's driving this fast. It's the best we can do."

"And how long do we have?"

"Two hours and two minutes."

"Two hours and one."

"Right," Angie said. She shut off the engine and took out the keys.

"We can make it!" Abba called.

"You're just hoping!" Angie yelled. "It's not real. You're saying that because you're cursed!"

"As we all are," Richard said. "As we always will be."

An eighteen-wheeler passed. The van shook slightly. Angie got out. She stood by herself on the shoulder. Some kind of black bird flew very high above her. It hovered and then, all at once, it tucked in its wings and dove downwards at a sudden great speed. It was, she knew, at least worth trying. Getting in the passenger door, Angie sat in the seat and dangled the keys towards Kent.

"No way," Lucy said.

"I'd rather be cursed than dead," Richard said.

"Really?" Abba asked him.

"That is a very bad idea."

"Does anyone have a better one?"

"What?" Kent asked, belatedly realizing that he'd become the centre of attention.

"Kent," Angie said. She tossed him the keys. He almost caught them. Bending over he picked them up off the floor. Angie waited until he sat back up. "It's all up to you."

"Yes! *Fucking* yes! I can do this!" Kent said. He crawled between the seats and behind the wheel. He adjusted the chair and the mirrors. Angie buckled her seat belt. Kent pulled onto the highway and they all clutched whatever was closest.

———

Kent drove as if he were still the backup quarterback on the high school team, looking for opportunities to pass. Seeing pockets of space that would soon be open, Kent steered towards them. This unnerved Angie, since all she saw were pickup trucks and minivans.

"Kent . . ."

"Just relax."

"Kent!"

"I got it, I see it. I got it."

Repeatedly missing front and back bumpers by inches began to overwhelm Angie. She couldn't remember if the seat belt was supposed to go over her stomach or underneath it. Neither felt right. She knew Paul would have known.

"Damn it, Kent!" Angie said. "That was close. Really close."

"It's okay," Kent said. For a second he looked at her. His eyes were confident. He looked like the brother she used to know. "Why don't you close your eyes for a bit?" he asked. Angie closed her eyes. The van slipped to the left and the right. The swaying continued but her fear of it diminished. Soon she felt like they were in a boat, a tiny boat, like a lifeboat. The motion became soothing, like she was being rocked, and she fell asleep.

A LACK OF MOVEMENT WOKE Angie up. She opened her eyes and the first thing she saw was a stoplight. She saw that it was red. Then she saw the downtown intersection they were stopped at.

"We're in Vancouver? We're here?" Angie asked.

"We're close!" Abba said.

"Not that close," Lucy said.

"Close enough," Kent said.

The light turned green. Kent depressed the gas pedal and they were all pushed back in their seats. "Eight minutes," Abba called. Lucy pointed out the direction of the hospital. Kent cut off a taxi. He turned left in front of a fast-moving cement truck. He ignored the flashing lights of a crosswalk. He ran a yellow light. And then they were in front of the Vancouver and District General Hospital.

"Where should I park?" he shouted.

"Six," Abba said.

"Right there . . ." Richard said.

"But that's a disabled spot."

"So we get towed!"

"Right, right," Kent said and with surprising grace he pulled in. Every door of the van opened at once. They ran towards the hospital.

"Five."

"Let's go! Let's go!"

Neither Richard nor Lucy nor Abba nor Kent looked back as they raced towards the automatic doors. Angie was only halfway there as they disappeared through them. Forgiving them instantly, she kept going. When she reached the lobby, they were nowhere to be seen. She pressed the up button. The elevator doors opened immediately. Inside it was quiet. It stopped on the second floor. No one got on. The doors closed. When they opened again Angie stepped onto the fourth floor.

To her right was a door marked Stairwell #12. From behind it she heard an upward avalanche of footsteps. The door was flung open and they all burst through it.

"One minute!" Abba called.

"Angie!"

"This way," Angie said. There was a wheelchair beside the elevator. Richard put Angie in it. He pushed her as they ran down the hallway.

"Thirty seconds."

"Which way?"

"Turn right. It's up there."

Angie held on to the arms of the chair. They ran past orderlies and visitors. They ran as fast as they could.

"Faster!"

"That way!"

"Twenty!"

The door to Room 4-206 came in sight. Richard's chest heaved. Sweat poured down Abba's and Lucy's faces. They continued running. They ran faster still.

"Five . . . four . . . three . . ."

Kent was a step ahead of them. He stretched out his arms towards the open door.

"Two . . . one!" Abba said and two seconds later they burst through the doorway and inside their grandmother's hospital room.

"You're late," the Shark said.

These were her last words. Her eyes rolled back in her head. Her body went limp. The lights in the room dimmed. The television sets lost reception. She fell backwards against the bed. The machine made a high-pitched whine. The Shark's chest rose and it didn't fall. Then a red bolt of lightning slowly rose out of it. The bolt stretched up to the ceiling. Then it coiled itself and hovered over her heart. The tip, snake-like, searched left and right and then Richard stepped forwards.

"Me," Richard said. He looked over his shoulder at his brother and sisters. "If this doesn't work, get ready to run."

Richard turned back towards the lightning, which was already shooting towards him. It struck his chest. He gasped. He fell to his knees. He put his hands over his heart. And then he crumpled over.

Kent, Lucy and Abba ran towards the hallway. Abba didn't make it. The lightning exited through Richard's back and caught her ankles. It twisted around her legs. It coiled upwards, over her stomach. It covered her face. Then she fell to the floor.

The lightning shot into the hallway. Lucy had turned left. It caught her, easily. It went straight through her. In mid-air it stopped and it turned around and it struck her again. The lightning went through her six more times, as if she were a button being sewn on a shirt. Lucy fell forwards. She did not put out her hands to break her fall.

Kent had turned right. He looked over his shoulder and saw it coming. It gained on him, quickly. At the end of the hallway he stopped. He turned around and faced it.

"Stay the *fuck* away from me," Kent screamed. The lightning shot down his throat. His fingers stretched open. He balanced on his toes. Then his body slumped onto the freshly washed floor.

The lightning turned. It moved slowly through the air. Angie stepped into the hallway. The lightning stopped in front of her. Shades of red, from rust to ruby, shimmered from its tail to its tip. Angie raised her hands. She opened her palms.

"Please don't hurt the baby," Angie said. It darted into her.

BOOK FOUR:

THE
      L OVE
MOTEL

Paulette's shoes remained on her hands, not her feet, and Angie took a very deep breath. They stayed at opposite ends of the front hallway. Paulette twisted her wrists until the toes of her tiny pink runners were pointed directly at her mother. Angie had planned to be at the daycare by nine. It was now just before ten. The shoe fell from Paulette's right hand. It bounced on the second-hand carpet. Angie bent her knees until she was eye level with her daughter.

"Okay, baby. It's time to get your shoes on."

"No."

"It's not a choice. Put your shoes on."

"No!"

"Paulette Annie Weird-Waterfield! You put your shoes on now!"

"No!"

"Now!" Angie yelled. She instantly regretted doing this.

"B . . . ut . . . you said . . . we'd get . . . new shoes!"

"We will. I promise. Tomorrow. Today we're already late. We just need to get to daycare."

"I . . . want . . . to . . . stay . . . w . . . ith youuuuuuu."

"Come on, baby. Just get your shoes on. Please?"

"No!" Paulette yelled. She threw the other shoe off her hand. It landed on the carpet. The lights embedded in the soles began to flash.

"All right," Angie said. "Then I will help you."

Standing up Angie plucked a shoe from the floor. She sat down and held Paulette in her lap and tried to wedge the small shoe on her daughter's small foot. But Paulette pointed her toes, making it impossible to get her foot all the way inside.

"New shoes! New shoes! New shoes!" Paulette yelled.

"Fine!" Angie yelled. She threw the shoe. She did this in exactly the same way her daughter had. It landed on the carpet. The coloured lights started blinking again.

For Angie, the challenges of motherhood were many. The worst of which wasn't the whining, or the lack of sleep, or the constant colds, or the twenty pounds on her frame that wouldn't go away. It was that her daughter daily demonstrated the worst characteristics of herself. This, Angie had been unable to forgive.

Paulette wasn't alone in being out of her mother's good graces. Just this morning Angie had been unable to forgive Paul for leaving his cereal bowl on the table. She still hadn't forgiven him for losing their daughter's health card. Or for making so little money that they had to live in a basement apartment. Nor had she had forgiven her siblings for doing nothing but sleep—oh, call it a coma if you want, but that's what they were doing. She couldn't forgive them for making her live with a man she was no longer sure that she loved. Or forcing her to raise her daughter in a city she didn't particularly like. Angie could not forgive them for taking her life and making it all about them.

It had been almost three years since Angie had forgiven anyone for anything.

"You . . . said . . . we 'd g . . . et . . . new . . . shoes!"

"Don't be a crybaby," Angie said.

"But . . . you p . . . romised," Paulette said, snuffling. "You promised."

"I know. We will. Honest."

As Angie tried to control her breathing, the phone rang.

"Thank God," Angie muttered.

She found the phone in the kitchen. It was not on the charger. She did not forgive Paul for this. The caller ID said that it was the Vancouver and District Hospital. "Hello?" Angie asked. She listened. She held the phone tighter. "Yes, I'll be there as soon as I can." She rushed back into the front hallway. She found Paulette humming to herself. Her shoes were on her feet. But Angie couldn't forgive her for not putting them on when she'd asked the first time.

W

LUCY OPENED HER EYES. Thinking that the hospital ceiling was the hospital floor, she automatically reached out her hands, squeezed her eyes shut and turned her face away. A full second passed before Lucy realized that she wasn't moving. She reopened her eyes. Her arms remained outstretched and she saw the intravenous needle that was taped to the inside of her elbow.

Sitting up caused her shoulder-length hair to fall over her face, but Lucy didn't think much about this. She tucked it behind her ears. She picked at the clear plastic tape on the inside of her elbow. She tore it off her skin. She pulled the needle from her arm. Then she looked up. There were three other beds in the room. Abba was to her right. Richard and Kent were across from them. They all seemed to be sleeping, so her immediate concern became how thirsty she was.

Sliding out of bed made every muscle in her body ache. Her legs were stiff. She took tiny steps across the room. The door that she hoped was the bathroom was locked. She knocked as hard as she could, which wasn't very hard.

"Hello?" Lucy asked. Her vocal chords produced almost no sound. No response. She shuffled out of the room. The hallway was empty. At the end of it she turned right. Then she saw an orderly.

"I need to get a drink," Lucy said.

"Pardon?" the orderly asked. He took a step closer to her. "Water!"

"There's a kitchenette right around the corner, on the left."

Lucy moved as fast as she could. The orderly followed her. Without asking, she opened a cupboard, took out a coffee mug and turned on the tap. She did not let the water run so it could get cold. She filled the mug. She drank it, quickly. Water spilled down her chin. She refilled the mug: she drank it, too. She filled it again. It was only as she started to drink her fifth mug of water that she realized she'd had to ask for directions.

Richard sat up in bed and looked at the needle in his arm. He ran his index finger over the tape that held it in place. His eyes followed the translucent tube that ran from the needle to a clear plastic bag hanging from a tall steel cart. He followed the tube back down. His shoulder-length hair fell over his face. He pushed it out of his eyes without giving it much thought. He looked at the inside of his elbow. He stared at the needle. He stared at it for some time. He could not decide whether it was safe to remove it or not.

This caused him to emit a laugh larger than he ever had.

———

The second Abba's eyes opened she felt the absence of an incredible weight. She looked around the room and she was only slightly surprised to see Richard in the bed directly across from her. He said nothing, but he leaned towards her, expectantly waiting to hear what she was going to say.

Abba remained silent. She hoped that she wasn't about to disappoint her eldest sibling. This hope, almost immediately, vanished. Abba had never experienced this before. She realized that the incredibly heavy thing she no longer felt was the collected mass of a thousand hopes she'd never been able to let go of.

"Hope is worry's twin," Abba said, her voice thin and weak, "and both are useless."

Kent opened his eyes. He saw Abba and Richard dancing and singing in the middle of the room. He heard a door unlocking and then he saw a nurse rush out of the bathroom. It was at this moment that Lucy skipped into the hospital room, closely followed by an orderly. The orderly stood by the door as if on guard. The nurse ran into the hallway to find the doctor. Lucy joined the circle of Abba and Richard. Kent stayed in his bed. He looked down at his hands. They were in fists. He stared at them for some time. Then he relaxed his grip, spread his palms flat against the bedsheet and looked up at the orderly's massive face.

"Thank you for coming," Kent said.

"Okay?"

"I'm sure that taking care of us has been a chore. On behalf of all of us, let me thank you for your efforts."

"You're welcome?"

"I feel unbelievably good. Stiff, for sure. But overall, well, how can I put this?" Kent stopped. He pushed his hair out of his eyes and began to pick off the clear plastic tape.

"Don't do that . . ."

"It's okay. Thank you for your concern. I have to tell you that I find myself, how *do* I put this? Perhaps for the first time in my life I find myself with nothing to prove," Kent said. He removed the tape and pulled the needle out of his arm. Getting out of bed he took tiny steps towards his dancing siblings. Lucy and Richard let go of each other's hand and Kent joined the circle.

"I think the Shark really did it!"

"I'm free!"

"We're all free!"

"We're *fucking* free!"

"We're fucking free," they began to sing, their voices rusty and off-key. "We're all *fucking* free!"

W

ANGIE STEPPED INTO THEIR hospital room and her siblings did not stop doing their awful dance or singing their awful song, and she was unable to forgive them. Their green gowns had come undone at the back, so at least one bare ass was always pointing directly at her as they danced. She remained by the door and she didn't join them. Some time passed.

"Angie!" Richard called, finally.

"Hey! I can't believe that phone number is still on your arm!"

"That's where you are!"

"Yup," Angie said. She sat on Kent's bed. "I'm right here."

They let go of each other's hands. They started taking tiny steps across the floor. Angie stayed on the bed. The doctor arrived before they reached her. Lab-coated and serious he examined each of them. He shone a penlight in their eyes and put his stethoscope to their chests. He spoke of permanent damage to their muscles and brains. They laughed at each of these things.

"But we're fine!" Lucy said.

"We're better than fine! We're great!" Richard said.

"We're the best we've ever been," Kent said. "Ever!"

"Watch this," Abba said and she began to twirl. The others started twirling as well.

"I admit," the doctor said, "you all seem fine." He put his penlight back in his pocket. He made notes on his clipboard. His right foot was in the hallway when Richard stopped twirling.

"You didn't tell us how long we were out," Richard called.

The doctor's right toe tapped three times and then he turned around. "Over two and a half years," he said. He flipped through papers on the clipboard. "You were in a coma for . . . two years, eight months and twenty-seven days, to be exact."

Richard, Abba, Lucy and Kent looked at the doctor. They looked at each other. They started laughing, all four of them, all at once, laughing, together.

Sixty minutes later all five of the Weird siblings stood at their grandmother's grave.

"That's an awful lot of text," Richard said.

"I can barely read it," Abba said.

"She didn't even put her name on it," Lucy said.

"Or the date!" Kent said.

"What do you think it means?"

"It doesn't mean anything," Abba said. "It's absurd. Like life is."

"Don't be stupid! It means that you have to be brave enough to accept that some things in life aren't random. That they have meaning!" Angie said. Her siblings registered the presence of *the Tone*. They looked at Angie and then they looked at each other.

"You seem to know a lot about what the Shark was thinking," Lucy said.

"Yes you do," Richard said.

"Where is your baby?" Kent asked.

"Finally! And it only took you two hours to ask!"

"But where is it?" Abba asked.

"She. Paulette. She's at daycare. Paul's picking her up."

"I knew you two would work it out!"

"Don't get your hopes up. It's not working very well."

"Angie," Richard said. "I have to say, you sound bitter."

"And angry."

"A little sad."

"You sound like the Shark."

"Explain to us how it worked."

"How what worked?" Angie asked. She took a step backwards.

"The lightning went through us and then . . . ?"

"It went into me."

"Into, or through?"

"Into," Angie admitted, "it ended with me."

"Is that right," Richard said. Angie took another step back. Her siblings stepped towards her. They exchanged looks. They pounced. Before she knew it, Angie was flat on her back. Abba held down her feet. Richard held down her right arm and Kent her left. Lucy knelt beside her, her face inches from Angie's.

"We want our sister back," Lucy yelled, loudly.

"We need her! We need her back!"

"You had your chance! You decided to go!"

"Get out of her body you paranormal hag!"

"Stop it! Stop it! STOP IT!" Angie yelled. "I swear I am not the Shark!"

"Prove it," Lucy demanded. None of them loosened their grips.

"Lucy, those condoms you flushed down the toilet always washed back up. Kent, I once helped you bury shitty underwear in the backyard. Richard . . ."

"Okay, okay, we've heard enough," Richard interrupted.

"Wait. I want to hear what Richard did."

"Me too."

"What did Richard do?"

"There's something more, isn't there?" Richard asked.

"I'm afraid there is," Angie admitted.

"Tell us."

"It's big."

"Tell us anyway."

"Okay," Angie said. They let go and she stood up. She brushed grass off her coat. When every blade was gone, she brushed for a little while longer. Then she looked up at them. "When the lightning went into me, it said something."

"That happened to me too," Richard whispered.

"And me," Lucy said.

"Me too," Kent said.

"Yes," Abba said, nodding her head. "It spoke to me."

"What did she tell *you*?" Richard asked.

"It's bad, isn't it?"

"Yes," Angie said.

"Then just get it over with!" Kent yelled.

"She knew where Dad went."

"You mean like where his body is?" Richard asked.

"No."

"You mean . . ."

"I do."

"He's alive?"

"He faked it?"

"Yes," Angie said. She looked at her feet and tapped her heels together.

"Where is he?" Abba asked.

"He bought a house in Sydney."

"Australia?"

"Nova Scotia. On 98 Sampson Avenue."

"Did you go see him?"

"How is he?"

"What did he say?"

"I haven't gone yet."

"What?"

"Why not?"

"It seemed," Angie said and she took a very deep breath before she continued, "like something we needed to do as a family."

"I see your point," Richard said.

"Okay," Kent said.

"I agree," Lucy said.

"Is he still there?" Abba asked.

"Well, for obvious reasons the Shark's memories end a little over two and a half years ago," Angie said. "But as of that time, yes, I'm afraid that he was."

"Jesus," Kent said. No one said anything more. They could hear traffic, moving quickly.

"Can we get off her grave?" Angie asked.

They stepped off her grave. They reread the epitaph. Then, in single file, Richard, Lucy, Abba, Angie and Kent walked through the cemetery. Not one of them noticed that they'd arranged themselves in order of birth.

That night all five of the Weird siblings slept under one roof, and Paul and Angie slept in the same bed and neither of these things had happened in two years, eight months and twenty-seven days.

Angie and Paul slept on their sides, with most of the mattress between them. Angie couldn't fall asleep. "They want me to go with them," she said. Paul didn't answer for a long time and then he did.

"I know," he said.

"They're leaving in the morning."

"I think you should go."

"Nice."

"What?"

"Very supportive."

"It was supposed to be."

"You think I can just go?"

"How can you not?"

"Keep your voice down."

"Why can't you?"

"You think I'm just going to leave Paulette?"

"Angie," Paul said. He sat up. He didn't turn on the light. "It's not like you're going forever . . ."

"No."

"Are you?"

"It isn't the plan."

"You know that Paulette and I will be fine."

"I do," Angie said. She rolled onto her back.

"So if that's not it, what is it?" Paul asked. He reached out his hand, looking for hers. It landed on her breast. He decided to leave it there.

"It'll change me," she told him.

"What will?"

"Either way."

"If you find him or if you don't?"

"Yes."

"And you believe that, either way, it will take you away from here? From me? I'm not saying Paulette, but from me?"

"Aren't you worried about that?"

"Well," Paul said. He took away his hand. "I guess I'm kinda thinking, what with the way things are between us, it's worth the risk."

The next morning Angie woke up alone in the middle of the bed. She went into the bathroom. She washed her face. She scrubbed her forearm. The phone number remained perfectly legible. She tried to figure out what to do and she still hadn't made up her mind when she walked to the kitchen and found it crammed with Weirds.

Kent and Richard cooked pancakes. Paul poured coffee. Paulette sat at the kitchen table, between Lucy and Abba, who were teaching her how to shoot Cheerios from her spoon. Angie stood there and then she did something else she hadn't done in two and a half years—she started to cry.

"It's . . . s . . . o . . . goo . . . d to . . . s . . . ee y . . . ou all."

"Angie!"

"Morning!"

"How did you sleep?"

"Pancakes?"

"They're surprisingly good."

"I'll make you tea."

"Whatch tis," Paulette said. She shot a Cheerio at her mother. It hit her chest and then it fell and rolled under the table.

"Pretty good!"

"Aim a little higher next time."

"Aren't you g . . . oing to . . . m . . . ake . . . fun of me . . . for . . . c . . . rying?"

Forks became motionless. Juice glasses hovered mid-air. Pancakes cooled. They looked at each other and then they looked back at Angie. They realized that not only hadn't they done it, none of them had felt any need to.

———

During the forty-minute drive to the airport Paul and Angie talked only to Paulette. Her siblings were supposed to be following behind in a taxi, but Angie couldn't see them. Paul parked in front of the domestic terminal. Angie opened the back door of the Toyota and knelt down beside her daughter, who bounced in her car seat. "Wot are you bringing me?" she asked.

"What do you mean?" Angie asked. She picked off the Cheerio that was stuck to Paulette's chin.

"Daddy says that's why you go'n away. To get me a present!"

"Telling you would ruin the surprise."

"Tell me!"

"Well," Angie said. She grabbed the toes of Paulette's sneakers. "How about new shoes!"

"With lights!"

"These ones have lights."

"I know!" Paulette said. She kicked the back of the passenger seat and the lights in her shoes started to flash.

"I'll see you in seven days, maybe less," Angie said. She kissed Paulette's head. She closed the door, gently. On the sidewalk Paul held out her suitcase.

"You have to do this and you have to do it for real," he said.

"Bon voyage to you too."

"I'm really being serious, Angie. I think this is our last chance. I don't know what it is, but you need to find it."

"You may not like what I find."

"I know," Paul said. He leaned in to kiss her. She turned her head. He didn't kiss her cheek.

Angie watched them drive away. She could still see the Toyota when the taxi carrying her siblings arrived. It was a perfectly clean and dent-free cab. They'd rejected the first three that came along.

"How was the ride?" Angie asked. The Toyota turned left and was out of sight. She looked at her brother.

"Well," Richard said. He closed the passenger door. "He took us to the main terminal. So then we had to come over here to the domestic terminal."

"Interesting,"

"I thought so."

"Stop it!"

"It means nothing!"

"It means we're at another *fucking* airport!"

"I feel like we're living in airports!"

"None of you have been in an airport in almost three years," Angie told them. She picked up her suitcase. They picked up theirs. They all stepped through the automatic doors and inside the Vancouver International Airport where, without trouble, alarms or altercation, they boarded flight AC208 to Halifax, Nova Scotia.

AFTER FLYING FROM ONE SIDE of North America to
the other—an eleven-hour journey that included a stopover
in Ottawa—the Weird siblings stood in front of a baggage
carousel that was completely motionless. They'd all flown
first class. Richard had paid. Angie had been impressed with
the legroom, the entertainment system and the amount of
Scotch her sisters had consumed. Neither Abba nor Lucy
could support their own weight. As they waited for their
bags, Lucy leaned on Richard, and Abba braced herself
against Angie.

"Christ, it's 2:30 in the morning," Richard said. "I'm
gonna see if the car rental place is still open."

"I'll come with you," Kent answered.

Before Angie could protest Richard leaned Lucy against
her shoulder. She watched her brothers walk away. Lucy put
her arm around Angie's neck and tipped forwards.

"Hello, sister," Lucy said.

"Hello," Angie said.

"Not you. The other one. Hello—other sister."

A long pause followed. Lucy and Angie were convinced that Abba wasn't going to answer. Then she did. "Hello," Abba said. She leaned forwards so she could look at Lucy. Both of Angie's sisters were now literally hanging off of her.

"You know something about me, don't you?" Abba asked.

"Luce, ignore her."

"Maybe I do."

"Lucy. Seriously. This is not the time or the place for this."

"It's about me and it's not good and it's very important, isn't it?"

"It is."

"Why would you do this now?"

"It's very heavy you know, this thing that I know," Lucy continued. She leaned farther forwards. So did Abba. Angie took a step forwards so they wouldn't fall. "This thing that I know that you don't know that you're afraid of, is killing me. Having to hold it. It is not good."

"Then tell me."

"Look," Angie said. The yellow light on top of the machinery began to flash. The carousel started to spin.

"You are not . . ." Lucy said. She slipped, grabbed the back of Angie's neck and somewhat straightened herself. Black rectangular suitcases began circulating in front of them.

"Look! Lucy! Isn't that yours? What about that one?"

"You are not the queen of Upliffta!" Lucy said. She reached across Angie. She touched Abba, gently, on her cheek. "You are not the queen of anything."

"Then who is the queen?"

"Upliffta has no queen. It has been a republic since its inception. What year? I don't know. Long time ago."

"What about the castle? What about my husband?"

"Let's get into this at the hotel? Best to wait. Don't you agree?"

"From all reports a very beautiful man who loved you very much and wanted the world to see you as the princess he saw you as. As the queen he knew you to be! Very rich and very powerful. But no king," Lucy said. Straightening herself, Lucy stood without her sister's assistance. She raised her arms high over her head.

"Upliffta has no king!" Lucy shouted.

A small number of people turned and looked. Lucy kept her hands in the air. More bags tumbled onto the conveyor belt. More people pushed forwards to retrieve them. Space became limited. Lucy, her arms still raised, looked at Abba. But Abba silently watched the floor.

"That makes what the Shark said make sense," Abba said.

"Tell me! What did she tell you?" Lucy asked.

"You tell first!"

"She said to me, 'Being lost is the only way to get found.'"

"That's very poetic."

"I thought so. It's definitely helping. Now you tell me."

"She said, 'Your hope has trapped you—now you are free.'"

"You *were* trapped in hope," Lucy whispered.

"It gives me so much permission."

"It does. Permission granted! Wait. Permission to do what?"

"It's no longer up to me to keep hope alive."

"No longer needed!"

"I knew it was fake. But I hoped it wasn't. My hope stopped me seeing the truth."

"You are free to see truth!"

"It will not be my fault if our father cannot be forgiven!"

"No it won't be!"

"Upliffta has no king!" Abba shouted. She raised her arms over her head.

"Upliffta has no king!" Lucy repeated. She shook her fists at the end of her still raised arms. The people around them didn't look up. They pushed closer to the luggage carousel. Lucy and Abba turned and they lowered their arms and used them to hold each other.

"It won't even be my fault if they've lost our luggage," Abba said, which of course they had.

W

THEY WERE SURPRISED THAT IT TOOK them four and a half hours to drive from Halifax to Sydney: when they got there they were surprised by how much they hated it. A mothballed steel plant sat beside a used car lot. Tall buildings were rare. The houses needed paint. The people on the streets were missing both their teeth and their hope. The Weird siblings stared out the windows of their rented car, wondering how their father could have chosen this over them.

"It's like they don't have any zoning laws," Lucy said.

"It's not even a pretty ocean view," Abba said.

"Luce? Which way?" Richard asked.

Lucy stared at him blankly.

"Sorry, force of habit," Richard said, and then he stopped at a convenience store and asked for directions.

Sixteen minutes after crossing the city limits they parked in front of 98 Sampson Avenue. Angie looked at the house. Her heart fell. She'd wanted it to be a mansion facing the ocean, on a rocky cliff. What she saw was a split-level detached with a two-car garage.

"Maybe we should have called ahead?" Richard asked. He took the keys out of the ignition.

"Hello? Yes? Hey! It's us!" Abba said. "Your abandoned children? You remember us. We were just passing through . . ."

"Wanted to know if we could swing by?"

"For coffee and cake!"

"And explanations!"

"Perhaps even a little redemption?"

"If you have any," Kent said. He started to laugh. It had been a very long time since any of them had heard him do this. Lucy was the first to get infected. Quite quickly it became a bit manic. Their laughter would wind down. Then one of them would start again. The rest would follow. Angie feared that she might pee. Then she saw that the front door of 98 Sampson Avenue was starting to open.

"Oh shit," she said. She pointed. All laughter ceased.

He had thick silver hair. The wrinkles at the corners of his eyes were deep. He looked wise and also a little sad. He was everything they'd hoped their father would be, but he clearly wasn't Besnard. They decided to get out of the car, anyway.

"Hello?" Richard asked.

"Hello," he said. "Can I help you?"

"Of course. I mean, I hope so," Richard said. He looked at the ground. He looked back at the man who wasn't his father. "My name is Richard. Weird? We're looking for someone. We're looking for . . ."

". . . Besnard Weird," Abba offered. She hadn't interrupted Richard because he'd stopped talking, perhaps forever.

"Are you family?"

"We are."

"He said he had family. Back east. Are you from Trinidad?"

"We're from Toronto," Abba said.

"They both start with *T* and have three syllables," Angie said.

Using only her eyebrows Abba told Angie to shut up. Then she turned back to the silver-haired man. "Do you know where he is now?" Abba asked.

"I'm afraid that you're too late."

"Too late for what?"

"I'm so sorry, but you've missed him."

"Do you know where he's gone?"

"I'm afraid that Besnard's passed. Well, I guess, almost two years now."

They were not prepared for this. They froze. The man who lived at 98 Sampson Avenue froze too. Several moments passed and no one moved or spoke. Then the Weirds spoke at once.

"From what?"

"Did he ever talk about us?"

"What was he like?"

"Did he have other kids?"

"Was he happy?"

"I'm sorry," he said when their onslaught ended. "My son bought the house in an estate sale. I didn't really know him."

"It's okay," Angie said. "We didn't really either."

They watched him walk to his Toyota. They watched him get into the car and pull out of his driveway. Twenty minutes later they watched him drive back into it. The man got out. He did not address them. He began backing towards his home.

"Maybe," Lucy called after him, "you could give us directions to the cemetery?"

ON AUGUST 16, 2002, NINETY-ONE days after their father's funeral, the five Weird children were all home when the doorbell rang. Richard answered it. Lucy, Abba, Angie and Kent came with him. A courier stood at their door. None of them spoke to him. They had developed an aversion to couriers. Hand-delivered packages inevitably contained some form of lawyer-drafted notice that their house was another step closer to being seized by the municipal government of Toronto. But there were several things that made the envelope in this man's hand different. It was white, not brown. It was thin, not thick. And most striking was that the address was handwritten in a loose elaborate scrawl they recognized as their father's.

"Are any of you Weird?" the courier asked.

"I suspect you are as well," Richard said.

"Who hired you?" Lucy asked.

"Pardon me?"

"Who is sending us this envelope? Who's paying you?"

"Hengelo and Associates," the courier said, reading from his clipboard. "It's a law firm."

"That we know," Richard said, "only too well."

Hengelo and Associates had handled all of Grace Taxi's legal concerns. They had also administered Besnard's will. Richard nodded. He stepped forwards and he signed for it. The courier walked back to his truck and drove away. Richard balanced the envelope on the tips of his fingers. Then, cocking his wrist like he was throwing a Frisbee, he chucked it into the bushes beside the porch.

The rest of the evening went as usual, or at least what had become usual. Richard made three boxes of Kraft Dinner and they ate it. They turned on the television and watched it without changing the channel or paying any attention to it. Just before midnight Abba and Lucy carried blankets outside. It was their turn to sleep in the Maserati.

They'd left their father's car in the driveway, right where the tow truck had dropped it. The car had become an extension of the house, an extra room with a specific function, like the laundry room or the kitchen: the Maserati was where they went to grieve.

At least once a day each of them walked to the car and sat in the passenger seat. Some of them cried. Some of them shouted. They held long one-sided conversations with their father. They punched the dashboard. All of them would have slept in it every night, but there was only room for two, so they had to take turns.

———

Lucy and Abba closed the front door and went out to the car. All Angie could think about was the letter. She looked at the television. She looked at Richard. Richard looked at his hands. When he stood, Angie and Kent followed him outside. They searched the bushes. They couldn't find it. "I've got it," Lucy said. Her hand stuck out of the driver's side window. It held the thin white envelope.

Neither Lucy nor Abba complained as Angie, Richard and Kent squeezed inside and sat on top of them. They stayed like this for several moments before Angie pulled the envelope from Lucy's hand. Five minutes later Kent took it from her. He opened it. There was a single piece of paper inside, which Kent unfolded and read out loud.

"Dearest wife and children," Kent said. "There's always a discount box. The, in second. The word: attic. With of eternal, the wisdom coach, love house, Dad."

"Damn it, Kent! Let me do it."

"I did it right! That's what it says."

"Are you sure?"

"You think I can't read?"

Richard took the letter from Kent's hands. The paper trambled slightly as he read it. Then he crumpled it into a ball.

"No, wait, don't!" Abba said.

"It's gibberish. It's nonsense. It makes as much sense as his *fucking* death did."

"Kent's right."

"I think it's one of his stupid codes. Give it here," Abba said. Richard threw the balled-up letter. It hit Abba in the forehead. Using Lucy's arm, she smoothed it flat.

"There," Abba said. She passed the letter to Richard and pointed to every other word.

"Always . . . discount . . . the . . . second . . . word," Richard read out loud.

"It is a code," Lucy said.

"Just not a very good one," Richard said.

"It's almost insulting," Abba said.

"Explain it right now or I swear, I *fucking* swear . . ."

"Relax, Kentucky. Just be calm. Read every second word but start with the second one," Richard said and he passed the paper back to Kent.

"Always . . . discount . . . the . . . second . . . word . . . With . . . eternal . . . wisdom . . . Dad."

"Now do it again starting with the first word."

"There's a box in the attic of the coach house."

"I vote that we do not go find this box," Lucy said. "That it would honour his memory more not to go find it."

"How do you people come up with this *fucking* shit?"

"I didn't see it either," Angie said.

None of them moved. Then, all at once, they scrambled out of the car and ran inside the coach house. Standing in the spot where the Maserati would normally have been parked, they looked up at the small rectangular hatch in the ceiling.

"I didn't even know the coach house had an attic," Kent said.

"Are you still a virgin?" Lucy asked.

"Be nice to Kent."

"Are you?"

"Are *you*?"

"Enough," Abba said. Richard pulled a Zippo lighter from the front pocket of his jeans. He handed it to Angie.

"Why do I have to do it?"

"Because it's your role in the family," Richard said. The rest of them nodded. Angie put her hands on her hips. Then she took the Zippo and started up the ladder made of two-by-fours nailed to the wall. She pushed up the hatch. She poked her head into the attic. She flicked the Zippo.

"What do you see?' Richard asked.

"Camping equipment…"

"What else?"

"Christmas decorations…"

"And?

"Wait," Angie called. Her feet climbed up to the highest two-by-four. "This one's marked First National Bank of Rainytown."

"But Rainytown's in the house," Kent said. "And we never made a bank."

"Are you sure?"

"Definitely."

"Bring that one down," Richard said.

Angie grabbed it near the top and tugged it towards her,

but the box was much heavier than she'd expected it to be. It tipped over. Bundles of hundred-dollar bills spilled out of it. Money fell through the hatch and onto the floor of the coach house.

"Holy shit."

"Holy *fucking* shit."

"Jesus."

"Unbelievable."

"That's about half of it," Angie said. She pushed another armful of money through the hatchway.

They carried it inside the house and stacked it on the dining room table. They stared at the pile. None of them wanted to touch it. "It doesn't even seem like money anymore," Richard said. "Like when you say the same word so many times it loses its meaning."

"Where do you think it came from?" Abba asked.

"He never seemed like a planner to me," Lucy said.

"Maybe it came from those hoods?" Kent asked.

"Hoods?"

"You know, those shady-looking guys he only talked to in the coach house."

"Shady?"

"It does seem like an awfully large amount," Richard said, "to be acquired by legal means."

"In cash."

"In bundled hundreds."

"What if all this was planned?" Kent asked. "Just another stupid puzzle?"

"Don't even think about it," Abba said. They struggled not to think about it. The struggle was exhausting.

The money had been found shortly before midnight. It was three when Richard split it into two piles. The first was enough to pay off the back taxes. The second pile he began to divide into five.

"Make it six," Lucy said.

"Six?"

"One for Mom," Lucy said. "We'll need to take care of her too."

Richard divided the pile into six. When he was finished, he yawned. Kent and Lucy were already half asleep. Angie said good night. At the top of the stairs she quickly turned and saw that brothers and sisters were following her up. She didn't take a good look at them as they walked up the stairs behind her. For the next eight years she would regret not doing this.

The next morning both Abba and her stack were gone.

THERE WERE NO TREES in the Barkhouse Memorial Cemetery and the tombstones were close together. As they searched for row 23-B, plot #26, the light went grey. Then it began to snow. They walked deeper into the cemetery, the snow crunching under their feet. It was the only sound they heard.

The tombstones ended at row 75-A. Row 1-B started where the graves were marked with plaques, which sat flush against the ground. They walked to 23-B. Counting twenty-six plaques in, they semicircled their father's grave. Richard bent down and wiped away the snow.

"That's . . . a lot of text," he said.

There was no name or date. There was no mention of his children or his loving wife. It simply read:

I, truly, am finally still. Once alive now running joy, a memory motel, grateful, in united shell, a cove of . . . truth.

Richard bowed his head and folded his hands in front of him. Angie and Lucy began to cry. Kent held them both.

"Goddamn it!" Angie shouted.

"What?" Richard asked.

"He did it again!" Angie said.

"He did what again?" Kent asked.

"Oh my God!" Abba said.

"He kinda did it again," Lucy said.

"Why would he do this?" Richard asked.

"Come on! Someone please *fucking* tell me what's happening . . ."

"Read every second word, Kent," Angie said. Her face had gone white. She crouched down and put her head between her knees.

"Truly . . . finally . . . once . . . now . . . joy . . ."

"No, no," Angie said. She remained crouched. Her voice was muffled. "It only works the one way."

"It's like his letter," Abba said, quietly. "The money-trail letter."

"That's why I started with the second word."

"Start with the first word. Start with the 'I.'"

"Fuck!"

"There ya go."

"What is a shell cove?"

"It's Shell Cove."

"How could he do this?"

"Why would he do this?"

"Fuck!"

"Will somebody please tell me what Shell Cove is?"

"It's at the top," Angie said. She stood. The colour had not returned to her face. "It's right up at the top of Cape Breton. Near Meat Cove. We'll have to wait until tomorrow. We'll head out first thing tomorrow."

W

ANGIE COULD NOT LOOK AT THE tropical beach scene mural, which covered the entire wall, for one more second. She turned on her side and stared at the digital numbers of the clock radio beside her bed. They read 1:23 when she heard a knock. Angie sat up. She accidentally looked at the beach scene. She heard the knock again. It came from the door connecting the two rooms they'd rented at the Sydney Motor Court Motel.

"Are you awake?" Lucy asked. She was sleeping, or rather failing to sleep, in the bed beside Angie's. Abba failed to sleep beside her.

"No, I'm sleep staring," Angie said.

"Then get the door!" Abba said. "Please?"

Angie climbed out of bed. She unlocked the door. Kent and Richard came into their room. They were both fully dressed.

"Our motel room is making us crazy," Kent said. He sat on the end of her bed. "Nice fake sunset."

"It's not the room. It's the waiting," Richard said. He

stared at the mural. "Although that *is* atrocious."

"We haven't slept either," Angie said.

"Do you think we should just go?" asked Lucy.

"Why not?" Kent asked.

"I agree," said Abba.

"Okay then," Richard said, "let's."

Having no suitcases, as they'd left the Halifax airport before their luggage had been found, they had nothing to pack. They walked to their rented car. It was snowing, heavily. Richard started the engine. Angie worked the heater. Kent found the snow brush. He cleared off the hood and the headlights and the front and back windshields. Then he got into the back seat beside Abba and Lucy. There was snow on his boots and his shoulders and stuck in his hair.

"It's really coming down out there," he said.

"We'll be fine," Richard said and he reversed through the parking lot.

"But, really, it's pretty bad."

"We'll drive through it," Richard said, and for different reasons, they all agreed.

Six hours into a three-hour trip, all they could see was snow. The road wasn't visible. Neither was the shoulder. There was only white, which broke into an infinite number of snow-flakes moments before hitting the windshield.

"It's like they're suicidal," Richard said.

"Who?" Angie asked.

"The snowflakes," Richard said. "They keep hitting the windshield. How could there be so many of them?"

Richard loosened his grip on the steering wheel. He tightened it again. He leaned back in the driver's seat and then he leaned forwards. They'd already turned onto the Cabot Trail, which should have taken them into Shell Cove. But then the weather had gotten even worse. Now their top speed was 20 km/h. It often went down to 10. They kept driving because it seemed slightly safer than pulling over. No one spoke. The windshield wipers were loud. Then Richard cleared his throat. This was a gesture Angie had never heard him make before.

"Angie," Richard said, "I just want to say that I'm sorry."

"Okay," she said.

"No, really, I'm serious. I want you to hear this. I'm sorry."

"I said okay."

"I'm very serious . . ."

"Keep your eyes on the road."

"Are you listening to me?"

"If I promise to listen will you keep your eyes on the road?"

"Yes."

"What are you sorry about, Richard?"

"All of it. Everything. Angie . . ."

"Eyes. On. The. Road."

"Angie, none of us knew about the curses, not for sure, but we kinda did. You know?"

"I know."

"So we all knew about you and the forgiving thing. That you'd forgive us for anything we did to you."

"I know that you're sorry."

"All those horrible things I made you do because I knew you'd forgive me. All of it. Not just the chores. But making you lie for me and cover things up. All the other shit I don't even want to say. I took advantage of you and I'm so sorry about all of it," Richard said. He kept his eyes on the road but he took his right hand off the wheel. He reached across the space between them. He squeezed Angie's arm.

"It's okay."

"Is it?" Richard asked. The snowflakes continued hitting the windshield. Richard kept his hand on her shoulder. Angie heard seat belts unfasten and then the rest of them crowded behind her seat. They each touched her shoulder and gently squeezed. "Do you forgive me?"

"And me?"

"Me too?"

"All of us?"

"Ah, you guys. You don't know how much I want to. I really, really want to," Angie said.

"But you won't?"

"I am unable to," Angie said and it didn't seem so bad when she said it like that. It just seemed like four words and not like something that had made the last two and a half years the worst of her life.

"Turns out that my blursing," Angie said, "may have been more blessing than curse."

"Angie, that's awful," Abba said.

"You haven't been able to forgive anyone at all?" Lucy asked.

"Not in all this time?" asked Richard.

"*Fuck*," Kent said. No one said anything else. They didn't have a chance to. It was at this point that the car, while going downhill, hit a patch of ice and spun out of control.

IT WAS NOT SLEEP BUT IT WAS something very much like sleep and Angie was deeply within it when the thought forced its way into her mind that the engine might still be running. She tried to open her eyes but they were locked. She listened. She heard the wind and the windshield wipers and then faintly, behind all those other sounds, the sound of a running engine. This impressed her. It was obviously a good engine if it could keep running after an accident. But then she thought that maybe this was a bad thing.

She was almost positive that after they'd flipped onto their side they'd slid backwards and suddenly stopped. Maybe a snowbank? She could remember a made-for-TV movie where this couple got into a car accident and their tailpipe was blocked by mud and they died from carbon monoxide poisoning and she was pretty sure that snow probably worked the same way. So she tried to open her eyes but they were cement. She waited. She tried again. Then they were open and she saw the keys dangling from the ignition but the distance between them and her made her eyes close.

When she finally got them open she got confused because gravity was coming from the passenger door. But, regardless, never mind that, the keys were still very much too far away. She looked at her brother, at how his body slumped against the seat belt. Then she didn't want to look at him. She looked at the floor, which was presently the passenger window and there was Richard's cellphone. HOORAY! She put it to her ear. She said, "Help us," and then she remembered that she'd have to dial a phone number and this almost broke her. Putting numbers in sequence seemed mystical and baffling and it made her head droop and that's when she saw her forearm and there they were, ten of them, already sequenced. HOORAY! Slowly and carefully and with very much effort she dialed the numbers written in Magic Marker on her forearm. The phone began to ring and on the third ring the ringing stopped.

—Hello?

—How are you?

—Who is this?

—It's okay. You don't have to know us. I can't forgive. But I'm not calling about that. I'm only calling because my grandmother wrote this number on my arm before she died and now we're about to die because we've had an accident on the road to Shell Cove. I don't even know which one. Cape Breton! Carbon monoxide! How far away? Can't say. Last place I remember is Capstick! Rhymes with lipstick! But we're serious to die if not soon discovered. No joke, she said, which made her laugh and she wasn't sure whether she laughed outwardly or just inside but her eyes closed again and this time she could not, for the life of her, get them open.

W

THE PILE OF SNOW ON THE carpet was four inches deep and just below the foot of the bed Angie woke up in. The room's only window was open. Large, slow-moving snowflakes flew over her head. Each one cut a different path through the air but they all landed on the pile, making it grow. Watching this was calming. Angie could see her breath, but she didn't feel cold. Every surface in the room was dusted with an undisturbed covering of snow. Angie took in all of these things and she began to suspect that she was dead.

Her suspicions were not lessened when she sat up. She was underneath seven woollen Hudson's Bay blankets. On the opposite wall was a framed nail-art picture of a schooner. The room was filled with mass-produced furniture from the eighties. Should there have been an afterworld specifically created for the Weirds, it would look like this.

Her suspicions became a conviction when she looked out the window. At the edge of the parking lot was a sign. Through the snow the words *l ove Motel* shone in red neon. Angie couldn't explain the space between the *l* and the *o*. But she reasoned that for all her earthly sins and sufferings, an eternal reward in something as unglamorous yet pleasurable, comfortable yet transitory as a love motel seemed perfectly appropriate.

The door connecting her room to the one beside it was open. Struggling from under the blankets Angie stepped around the pile of snow. She walked through the door. There was a pile of snow in the middle of this room too. There were two beds. In the one closest to the door was Kent. In the other was Richard. Both were awake. Neither seemed surprised to see her.

"Are we dead?" Kent asked.

"I think we are," Angie answered.

"We aren't dead," Richard said.

"How do you know?"

"I feel normal."

"But normal is what dead would feel like to dead people," Angie said.

"Good point," Richard conceded.

"Do you think this is heaven or hell?" Kent asked.

"Maybe both?"

"It's neither," Richard said but his voice was defensive. "It's just some tacky motel."

"The Love Motel?"

"You mean the l ove Motel."

"So?"

"You believe in God but you don't think he can spell?"

"Good point," Angie conceded. "But what about the snow? There's a pile back in my room too."

"I don't know about that. I agree it seems odd."

"It's very peaceful."

"That it is."

"What do you think's in there?" Kent asked. He nodded towards the door into the next room. It too was open.

"We are," Abba called.

Angie led the way. She noticed that each of her feet wore three pairs of heavy wool socks. Richard and Kent wore three pairs of wool socks too. Together, they entered the next room. There was another pile of snow on the floor and two more beds. Lucy was in one and Abba was in the other.

"I agree that we're dead," Abba said.

"Don't be so stupid," Lucy said.

"Vote," Kent said. "Who thinks we're dead?"

Angie raised her hand. So did Kent and Abba. The door to the motel room opened. They all turned and looked. Snow and wind entered the room and then, so did their father. Angie, Kent and Abba lowered their hands; Richard and Lucy thrust theirs into the air.

THEY STARED AT THEIR FATHER. Angie, as they all were, was stunned by how little shock seeing him caused. The thinning hair and stooped shoulders and the large black circles under his eyes weren't just disappointing. They were demystifying. The longer he stood there the more human he became.

"Did we . . . die?" Richard finally asked.

"Almost. Yes, definitely, almost," their father said.

"Did you save us?"

"How did you find us?"

"The RCMP called," he said. He shut the door and kicked snow off his boots. "From Vancouver. They said some crazy old lady in the hospital called them, claiming that some crazy woman called her from a snowstorm near Shell Cove. Guess I was the closest. Closest with chains on my tires, anyway. Damn near didn't go."

"What's with the name?" Angie asked.

"What?"

"The Love Motel. Why are we in the Love Motel?"

"Jesus. That's what you want to know? It was the Shell Cove Motel when I bought it. Then the *s* burnt out and that sure didn't help business. So I took out the *h* and the *e* and the first *l* and the *c*."

"The Love Motel."

"The l ove Motel."

"It's good. We have people coming all the way up from Halifax. The view off the cliff's pretty, so no one really cares what it's named."

"And the snow?" Richard asked.

"It's just a storm."

"Why is it in the rooms?"

"Ventilation," he said. The aggravation in his voice sent a rush of nostalgia through them all. "You almost died from carbon monoxide poisoning. You needed fresh air and lots of it. I bundled you up best as I could but it was touch and go from there. Didn't know you'd woken up yet. For a second there I thought you were all ghosts!"

He pointed to the mirror above the wardrobe. They all turned and looked. Snow was caught in their hair and clothes. Their skin was grey from the poison. They did look like ghosts. They looked back at their father. He didn't move towards his children. They didn't move closer to him.

"Why aren't you kids more angry?" he asked.

"Maybe we're dead," Lucy said.

"It'd be easier if you were just angry. Go ahead! Get angry! Let me have it."

"We've been having a lot of epiphanies lately," Abba said.

"I'm not even sure if seeing you is the most improbable thing that's happened to us recently," Kent said.

"We're just amazed to see you alive," Lucy said.

"Well you almost didn't get the chance," their father told them.

"But we did," Richard said. "We found you. You found us!"

"Wait," Angie asked. She took a step backwards. "What do you mean?"

"Don't any of you know what day this is?" Besnard asked.

"I'm not exactly sure what year this is . . ."

"January 22?" he asked. Exasperation returned to his voice. His children shrugged their shoulders. "It's my *fucking* birthday! I turn fifty-three today."

"Don't say it, Dad," Angie said. "Please please don't say it."

"Don't say what?" Lucy asked.

"Angie, listen to me," her father continued, "what I'm about to say is very serious."

"Please? Don't say it."

"What don't you want him to say?"

"It's not the year. It's that I'm in the terminal stages of pancreatic cancer. My pain is constant."

"Don't you want to live to be at least a hundred?"

"I've fought it long enough. I was born at 7:17 p.m. on January 22. I will die at 7:17 p.m. on January 22. Not a second later or a moment earlier . . ."

"Who doesn't love a countdown?"

"Angie!"

". . . a little over three hours from now. I can only believe that this is no coincidence. That something divine and uncanny has brought you here, at this moment."

"Until you realize coincidence doesn't exist . . . "

"Stop it, Angie!"

"Shut up!"

"The biggest mistake of my life was abandoning you all. It felt right at the time. At least it felt like a solution. Then it didn't, but there was no going back."

"Please don't ask, Dad. Please don't ask."

"In three hours and twenty-odd minutes I'll be dead. I would like nothing more, my final request, what would allow me to go with peace and dignity, is for all of you to forgive me."

Besnard began to cough. The coughing turned into a fit. He took a plastic bottle from his pocket. He twisted it open. As he poured yellow pills in his open palm he coughed again. The pills flew into the air. Angie was out the door before they landed.

W

IN SOCK FEET ANGIE'S options were few. The storm remained strong and the parking lot was buried. But the roof of the motel had an overhang, which had created a small snowless trench against the side of the building. She ran along this because there was nowhere else to go.

Angie ran the length of the motel. Then she ran alongside of it. Her feet were already cold. When she got to the back she saw her father's 1947 maroon Maserati half-buried in the snow.

The car was parked with the driver's side against the back wall of the motel. The front end faced her. It was still buckled. The basketball-sized hole remained in the front windshield. A flattened cardboard box had been duct-taped over the passenger window. Angie easily removed this and then, headfirst, she crawled inside.

The sound of the wind disappeared but snow blew through the open window. She moved over and sat behind the wheel. She watched her breath. A pile of snow grew on the passenger seat. She had no idea how much time passed and then

Richard arrived. He put his head through the passenger window. She didn't look over.

"Amazing. He must have had it towed," Richard said. "Can I come in?"

"It's your funeral."

"Funny."

Richard pushed in several blankets and then he climbed, feet first, into the car. Angie put her hands on the wheel. She continued to look through the hole in the windshield.

"Here," Richard said. He held up one of the blankets. "Freezing to death will not help you make your point."

Her teeth were chattering. She took it from him. Richard put several more on top of her.

"How much time is left?" Angie asked.

"You've been out here about an hour."

"And I suppose you've all forgiven him already?"

"Before we'd even noticed you were gone. Sorry."

"Do you think he's really going to do it?"

"He's not well," Richard said. His voice had cracked. "Yes. I believe he'll pull it off."

"I don't think I can do it."

"It's true, you're in a hard place," Richard said. He extended his index finger and he wiped a line of snow from the dashboard. "Angie, I've spent my whole life trapped in the future. I can tell you that it's just as dangerous as being trapped in the past."

"And?"

"It won't hurt you to forget what he did. Or at least if it does, you'll heal. Sometimes it's important to let yourself get hurt. And right now, the present tense is that our father is in there and he's sick and weak and dying. That's all you need to remember."

Angie nodded her head. She didn't look over. Richard sat there for several moments and then he wrapped a blanket around her feet and crawled back out the window. Angie sat in the car. She lost track of time. She continued staring through the hole in the windshield, even when Abba crawled through the passenger window.

"Hey," she said.

"Hello."

"I'll go right now if you drink this," Abba said. Angie looked over and saw that Abba held out a Thermos. It was the old-fashioned kind, plaid and metal. Abba unscrewed the top and poured what appeared to be chicken soup into the upturned lid. She held it out. Angie took her hands out from under the blankets and held it. She kept her hands wrapped around the upturned lid because the heat felt so good.

"Can I just say one thing before I go?"

"Will you say it anyway even if I say no?"

"Yes."

"Go ahead."

"The thing about hope, it's clear to me now, is that it isn't noble or saintly. It's something you do for yourself. That's why it's so easy to get trapped in it," she said.

"So?"

"Maybe forgiveness works the same way? Maybe it's easier to do than you think," Abba said. She reached out her hands and put them on Angie's and then she raised the mug to her sister's mouth. Angie drank a bit of the soup. After the first sip she started drinking it on her own.

"Our father has been a ghost for most of our lives," Abba continued. "This is your last chance to get rid of him. Don't let your anger at him stop you from doing something for yourself."

Angie drank the last of the soup. Abba refilled the mug. She put the lid on the Thermos, which she left on the seat as she crawled out the window.

"How much time is left?" Angie asked.

"A little over an hour," Abba said. She crouched down and looked through the passenger window. "Are you sure you want to stay out here? Your lips are a little blue. You could just as easily not forgive him inside, where it's warm."

Angie shook her head. She listened to Abba's footsteps. She wondered who'd be next. The snow had built up on the dashboard when Kent climbed inside the car. He sat down and then he reached underneath him and pulled the Thermos between his legs.

"Can I have some of this?" he asked.

"Go ahead," Angie said. Kent unscrewed the top. He drank straight from the Thermos. Angie held out her mug and he filled it.

"So what's your argument?"

"Strength!"

"Is there more?"

"Physical strength is bullshit. Emotional strength is gold. Don't be weak—forgive him!"

"Kent, that's the lamest one yet."

"Well, ya, but this really isn't my thing. And Lucy's coming up, so you know, you still got that. Can I tell you something though?"

"Of course."

"You wanna know what the Shark said to me?"

"Yes."

"She said, 'Only the weak are afraid to appear so.'"

"I don't know if that applies."

"Maybe it does. Maybe it doesn't. I just wanted to tell you. Can I tell you something else?"

"Sure."

"I love you. I really do," Kent said. Angie turned and she looked at him. His head was tilted back and he drained the last of the soup from the Thermos.

"I love you too," Angie said.

"I know," he said. "He's really going to do it. You've got about twenty-five minutes."

Then he crawled back out the window. Angie began to wait. She waited for a long time. She waited for what seemed like much more than twenty-five minutes. Then she heard Lucy's footsteps in the snow. Lucy climbed into the passenger seat. She did not turn to look at Angie. She looked straight ahead and then she started talking.

"No one gets found in love. Everyone gets lost in it. Because love is overwhelming. It's beyond your control. You have to relinquish control to be in love. And that's a good thing. There's a beauty to being lost in something bigger than you.

"The bad part is that you're now vulnerable to them. They can hurt you in ways that no one else can," Lucy said. She continued to look at the dashboard but her left hand reached out and took Angie's. "But here's the thing. Love is so uncontrollable that sometimes it won't go away, even when you want it to. Even if someone's hurt you really badly, you may still love them. That's what forgiveness is. It's admitting that even though they've done this horrible, horrible, thing, you still love them. If you cannot forgive someone, you're telling them you have no love for them. So ask yourself, quickly, is there any love for him inside you? If there is, then not forgiving him will be a lie. One you will never, ever, be able to take back."

Lucy let go of Angie's hand. She didn't wait for her sister to respond. She crawled out of the car and Angie sat there, alone.

MORE SNOW CAME THROUGH the window. The pile on the passenger seat grew. Angie's breath remained visible. She looked through the basketball-sized hole in the windshield. She waited for an epiphany but all she felt were her hands getting colder.

She sat there a while longer. Then she pushed off the blankets and crawled through the passenger window. Her siblings had all used the same set of tracks through the snow. She stepped in these as she walked back to the motel. The bell above the door dinged as she went inside. No one came to greet her. She walked around the counter. Sitting on a kitchen chair she pulled off the three layers of snow-encrusted socks. Her toes were white and wrinkled and it hurt to touch them.

"Angie?" Richard called.

"I'm here," Angie said. She stood up. Her feet had gone pins and needles.

"Come on!" Abba called.

"Hurry up," Lucy said.

"Four minutes. Four *fucking* minutes."

"Okay! Okay!" Angie said. She limped towards their voices. Outside his bedroom door she readied herself for the strange things she expected to see. But when she went inside the lights did not dim, nor did the furniture jump around. All she saw was a sick, frail man lying in bed, surrounded by his children. Each of them touched her as she moved past and sat on the edge of his bed.

"I'm scared," he said. He raised his hands and she took them.

"Don't be."

"You don't have to do this. It's a lot to ask."

"But I can. I do. I really do, Dad," Angie said. She looked up at her siblings, then back down at her father. She looked into his eyes. She had expected just to voice the words. But at this moment it became clear to her that the only thing powerful enough to transform people into brothers and sisters, mothers and fathers, is the ability to forgive each other. That what really gets handed down from generation to generation isn't blood or history, but the will to forgive.

"I forgive you," Angie said. Besnard Weird nodded his head. Then his eyes stayed open.

W

ANGIE HEARD THE SNOWPLOW before she saw it. She was sitting on a wooden chair at her father's kitchen table. The chair wasn't comfortable. She hadn't moved from it in several hours. She was the only Weird awake. The rumble got louder. She stood up as the snowplow went past. It shook the windows. A dip in the road made it look like it had gone over the cliff. Angie turned around and saw that her siblings were standing behind her. They had seen it too.

"I know what we should do," Angie said.

"I agree," Lucy said.

"Is it legal?" Abba asked

"Who cares if it's legal?" Richard said.

"I can't think of anything he'd want more," Kent said.

"Neither can I."

"For him or us."

"Exactly."

Wearing layers of their father's winter clothes, they went outside. There were only two shovels so they worked in shifts. They dug right down to the frozen ground. They cleared a path from the back of the motel, across the parking lot, over the road, to the edge of the cliff. When they were finished they were exhausted and hungry. They didn't rest and they didn't eat. They went back inside the motel and into his bedroom.

"Should we dress him?" Lucy asked.

"He already is dressed."

"No, but, like in a suit?"

"Does he have one?"

"Can you ever remember him wearing a suit?"

"That's the only thing I can remember him wearing."

"Let's just leave him like this," Angie said. "Let's remember him like this."

Kent did not ask to take a vote. He took his father's right foot. Abba got hold of the left. Richard and Lucy held the shoulders. Angie ran ahead. Moving chairs and plant stands, she cleared a path. They lifted their father from the bed and they carried him through the living room, around the counter and out of the motel. Their boots slipped in the snow. Their arms got tired. They carried him all the way to the crumpled Maserati.

It was easy for Kent to get through the passenger window. The opposite was true for their father's body.

"I have never known him not to want to get into this car," Abba said.

"I think we're going to have to use a bit of force," Richard said.

They used a bit of force. They got him through the passenger window and behind the wheel. Kent fastened the seat belt. He put the gearshift into neutral, he crawled out, and they all began to push.

It was easier once they got started. When they cleared the back wall of the motel Richard opened the driver's side door. He turned the steering wheel and they navigated the corner. They gained momentum through the parking lot. They glided across the road. But on the other side there was a slight incline, which stole their momentum.

"Harder," Angie called.

They pushed harder. Richard and Kent turned around and put their backs against the trunk. Their boots slipped in the snow. They kept pushing and the car crested the incline. Then it began to move on its own. The Weird siblings ran alongside of it. They kept a hand on it. At the edge of the cliff they stopped. The Maserati kept going.

The Weird siblings watched it fall. It fell with impossible slowness. Then it hit the frozen surface of the water. The crumpled front end cracked through the ice. The car bobbled three times. It fell flat. And then it floated.

"No way," Lucy said.

"No *fucking* way," Kent said.

"Right to the end," Abba said.

"I did not see this coming," Richard said.

"Just wait," Angie said.

They all held their breaths. The car slowly began to sink. When it was completely submerged, they all breathed out.

———

Sixteen hours after they sent the Maserati over the cliffs of Shell Cove, two years, nine months and two days after the death of the Shark, and thirteen years after Kent scored his first and only touchdown, they stood in front of the departures board at the Halifax Stanfield International Airport. The rental car had been returned. The information on the board hadn't changed for several minutes. Yet they continued to stare at it.

The board announced many flights. One to Vancouver departed in ninety minutes. Another left for Montreal in two hours. There was a direct flight to Toronto, where there'd be flights to Upliffta. But no tickets had been purchased. All five of them stood there. They stared at the board. Then the destinations shuffled downwards. A new flight appeared at the top. It announced flight AC468, to Winnipeg, Manitoba, which left in three hours.

All of them saw it. And all of them gasped. They shuffled closer together. They took each other's hands. They looked down from the board and then at each other.

"The winter there isn't nearly as bad as they say," Lucy said.

"I have nothing waiting for me in Montreal," Richard said.

"Upliffta has no queen," Abba said.

"I can tell Paul and Paulette to meet us there," Angie said.

"I can't go back to Palmerston Boulevard," Kent said.

They said nothing more. Single file, they walked to the ticket counter. As they stood in line Angie imagined buying a big house in a residential neighbourhood. The street would be tree-lined. The house would be old. It would occupy a corner lot. They'd move their mother in with them. They'd take care of her together. They wouldn't let her cut their hair. When she and Paul had a second kid, they'd buy the house beside it. And then as her brothers and sisters became mothers and fathers, and uncles and aunts, they would buy more houses on the street. They'd own every one, on both sides, at the end of their block. Their children would spill out onto the sidewalks, riding bicycles and accidentally breaking windows. A new generation of Weirds, loving each other and being loved. Weirdly being Weird and weirdly doing well.

This is exactly what happened.

ACKNOWLEDGEMENTS

The author wishes to acknowledge that *Born Weird* would not and could not have been written without . . .

Rolly Kaufman, Shirley Kaufman and Liz Kaufman—who are nothing like the Weirds.

Barry Miazga and Karen Miazga—who are also nothing like the Weirds.

Phoenix and Frida.

The brilliant insight and editorial compassion of Pamela Murray. RIP Veronica.

The foolhardy belief of Sam Hiyate.

The inexplicable affection of Scott Pack.

The incalculable contributions of Zach Picard, Ian Cauthery, Stephanie Domet, Angelika Glover and Stacey Cameron.

The financial assistance of The Canada Council for the Arts, Lamport-Sheppard Productions and New Road Media.

The infinite patience and indestructible honesty of Marlo Miazga. The best story I've ever read is the one we're living.

ANDREW KAUFMAN is the author of *All My Friends Are Superheroes*, *The Tiny Wife* and *The Waterproof Bible*. He was born in Wingham, Ontario, the birthplace of Alice Munro, making him the second-best writer from a town of 3,000. His work has been published in eleven countries and translated into nine languages. He is also an accomplished screenwriter and lives in Toronto with his wife and their two children.